Trusting Heart Reunion

Trusting Heart Reunion

DeLora Conley-Walls

THREE SKILLET

TRUSTING HEART REUNION, Conley-Walls, DeLora

First Edition

The Reunion Series, Book 1

 THREE SKILLET

www.ThreeSkilletPublishing.com

Cover by Farley L Dunn

ISBN: 978-1-943189-51-9

— 1 —

"JANE WAGGONER, you're a silly old fool."

Jane, nearing sixty, although she looked a decade younger, peered in the mirror, running her fingers through her hair. Still beautiful, with softly retouched tresses and only the barest of crowfeet, she'd kept a trim figure with a regular workout.

Her makeup was the problem.

Her hair had fought her at every turn of the brush, but she'd finally beaten it. Her mascara? Dried out. That was the first tube. The second? Blue instead of black. Then, thank the stars, at the very back, hiding from her, she found the third, black, like she needed.

Her bloodshot eyes? Don't even go there. Her eye drops had barely made any difference.

"Sheesh!" She grabbed her keys and her red

clutch and yanked the door open. She'd never make her lunch date now. At least it was only Peggy Lynn Johnson.

She hit the remote to unlock the car door, only to fumble her keys to the ground. She was tired, too tired. That same nightmare. Bill, his accident.

All he'd done was head out for the weekly paper. She'd continued dinner preparations, totally unaware he was dying a block away. Even the sirens hadn't triggered any real alarm.

How would she ever pick up those thirty-three shattered years?

"Well, girl, you can at least pick up these keys," she muttered, leaning down to snatch them with her carefully manicured fingers. If she hadn't figured this out in three years, she guessed she never would. It'd take a miracle from the past to make a difference now, or maybe God's finger on the clock of life, moving the hands back for about thirty-six months.

Yeah, that would do it. Thirty-six months, and she'd talk Bill out of going after that paper.

Jane climbed into her car and sighed, her finger resting on the start button, not yet willing to push it. The truth swept over her with a rush of clarity. It wouldn't have mattered. Talking Bill out of going out that morning wouldn't have made a difference. The heart attack would have happened at home or in the car.

She whispered her pain into the silence, "God, don't you care?"

She glanced up at the sky overhead, the endless blue laced with cotton candy clouds. It was beautiful. Despite her gritty eyes and troublesome mascara, there were good things about her life. The blue sky overhead, a good car to drive, and Peggy.

What would she have done without Peggy?

She pushed the button, smiling at the soft rumble of the engine as it came to life, then the small clicks and purrs as the car worked through its startup diagnostics. This was Bill's last gift to her. He laughed when she said she wanted candy apple red, telling her it was the color of a ridiculous female. She explained to him it was the color of love.

It was six months after he died that she placed her order. She had the dealer wrap it in a giant white bow in the center of the lot. It was his last gift, and he didn't even know.

"Thank you, Bill." She backed out of the drive and turned toward the Community Center. She would enjoy this day. She would be pleasant, even charming, and Peggy would know that she was over Bill's death, ready to move on with the rest of her life. She would. She would.

She didn't even have to wipe tears away on the way to the Community Center. It was three days since she'd last cried. That was an improvement.

Maybe, just maybe she was putting Bill's death behind her.

JANE TAPPED THE WHEEL, debating on whether

to leave the car running or kill the engine. She could afford the gas, but Peggy was normally as punctual as a pincushion, and Jane was hungry.

"Your car may be in the shop, Peggy Lynn," she growled, "and I don't mind picking you up, but you do own a cell phone. It wouldn't hurt you to text me, so I know what's going on."

She opened the door as she jabbed the ignition button—harder than she should—to stop the engine. The words of her favorite song died away, but Jane murmured the lyrics in her own variation. "Stop in the name of love, don't you know I'm waiting on you." Then she punched the words, "Peggy Lynn!"

She laughed at how clever she sounded, and she closed the door and pushed the button to lock the car. She looked around before moving toward the building. The Center was pretty. Even with all her moping that morning, she had to admit that. Flowerbeds lined the walks, and the giant oaks created ever-changing patterns of dappled light. Well, it ought to look pretty, she decided. That's why she paid such high taxes on her house, so the city can afford the water bill when the sprinklers turned on.

She took a deep breath and decided it would be cooler under the shade, not standing in the lot in full sun.

No more had she made it to the front of the car when she saw her friend coming out of the door, trailing a small group of her adult students. It was a pottery class, continuing education, definitely not for college age kids. It was mostly seniors that attended, that and the occasional young mother who needed a break from the joys of motherhood. Jane raised her hand to wave only to see her friend in a deep discussion with one of her students. She let her hand drop to shade her eyes before turning to the car. That was when she heard Peggy call to her.

"Jane, can you believe it, after all this time?" The words quivered with excitement.

"Believe what?" She turned, putting a smile on her face.

"Who would have ever thought he would have turned up here?"

"Who—" Jane started, but a very familiar voice interrupted her question.

"Me. They say a bad penny always turns up now and again. Well, here I am."

The interruption was laced with amusement, but it was the voice, deep and penetrating, that stopped Jane cold. She felt the temperature had jumped ten degrees, and she knew it had nothing to do with standing in the sun. That voice was a tidal wave from the past, an avalanche of explosive memories, and a dark tide threatening to overwhelm her.

The man at Peggy's side was as tall as she remembered, but his hair was now woven with silver. Those eyes, though. There was no mistaking those caramel eyes. Still, the voice had been enough. Even in the darkest night, over the most distant connection, she would know that voice. It belonged to the only man she had ever loved. Yet, it couldn't be him.

Her heart told her differently, though. It beat faster, just like all those years ago, threatening her with discovery, telling the world around her that Bill hadn't been the only man in her life. There had been someone else, and if she'd had the chance, if things had played out differently, then she and Bill might never have been . . .

She caught herself. No longer. At one time he was the only man she'd ever loved. Then, Bill had filled the void left by Tarzan, and her life had eventually come back together. Slowly, but eventually.

What was he doing here?

TARZAN, KNOWN WITHIN his family circles as Tres Juan, was actually Juan Cordello Rivera III. Growing up, all his friends had been mesmerized by Saturday afternoon television. Their favorite show had been Tarzan. Say Tres Juan quickly, and the outcome was inevitable. Tres Juan became Tarzan, and, naturally, being Jane, she was paired with him. Tarzan and Jane, the lords of the jungle.

At first it had put her off, but Cord, as he liked to be called, was very TDH. That was Tall, Dark, and Handsome. Half Hispanic and half Irish, he was dark-haired with lightly bronzed skin, and every teenage girl swooned when he walked by. Eventually, Jane had caught the bug, and they became a couple.

Now, after nearly four decades, they were back together once again.

"JANE, ARE YOU AWAKE?" Peggy had made it to the car by then, and she reached and rapped Jane on the forehead with her knuckles.

"Jane?" This time it was Cord who quizzed her, in that resonant voice, rattling Jane's bones . . . and her heart and lungs and kidneys, too, she supposed. She pulled herself together.

"I'm sorry, Peggy. Of course, I recognize him." She held her hand out. "Welcome, Cord Rivera." She heard her voice. Her words were little more than terse, and she refused to look him in the eyes. Why, oh, why was Cord here now?

"Don't you mean Tarzan?" Peggy laughed, her hair bouncing around her face.

Jane was furious. She wanted to grab Peggy's mahogany mane and yank those curls to get her attention. Cord was the last man her friend should be flirting with after how he'd treated Jane all those years ago.

"Don't be a flirt," Jane hissed, batting at Peggy's arm. "I do *not* want to be around this man." Her words went unheard, as Peggy laughed again, her chortling covering her friend's hissed command.

"Nice to see you, too, Jane." Cord gave her a slow and easy smile.

Good Lord, I hope he didn't hear that. Jane shuddered at the idea of having Cord around again, but she didn't feel the compulsion to be rude, either. Not with her heart going ninety miles an hour just at the sound of his voice. Good heavens! How could she be attracted to a man she hated so much?

It was only then that he took her hand. She'd forgotten she'd offered it. Forty years since they'd last touched, skin to skin, and the electric shock jolted her as hard now as it had then. She was certain he could see the fire she felt in her face. This was Texas, and spring in Texas could be very warm, but it was outright hot. And it wasn't the weather, she was sure.

Well, she wasn't going to let him win at this game. He had abandoned her, not the other way around. It wasn't her fault the world had fallen apart all those years ago, and besides, this was her town. Not his. His family were the rich ones all those years ago, and hers had barely grubbed by, but no longer. She and Bill had done well. They were respected in the community. She could beat Cord at his own game.

"It's good to see you, too, Cord Rivera." Jane gave him her brightest smile. She wouldn't let him see her emotions. They would remain masked. Too many years and memories had gone by to let a meeting like this reveal anything. "Good-bye, Cord Rivera. I expect you have things to do, and maybe we'll meet up again. However, Peggy and I have plans, and we have to run."

She shook her hand free, only then realizing she was shaking inside. She turned without looking him in the face and made it to the car in record time.

"Oh, look at you!" Peggy dropped into the car and put her hand on Jane's arm. "I think I saw sparks of romance out there."

"You did not." Jane barked the words, and she hit the start button and flipped the temperature to its lowest setting, closing her eyes as the fan came on high. "Don't even suggest that, Peggy Lynn."

"I invited Tarzan to lunch. Oh, *Cord*, I forgot. I invited *Cord* to lunch."

Jane looked to see a grin on her face. "Sure, said the Wicked Witch of the West." She pulled the lever into reverse, only to see a black Escalade in her rearview camera. "We're blocked in. Just hang on."

"Jane."

She looked to see Cord standing beside her car. With a groan, she toggled the switch and let the window slide into the door. "Yes?"

"If you ladies don't mind, I'll chauffer you in my vehicle. I'm not sure where we're going."

"Do something, Peggy," Jane hissed, glaring at her friend.

"Sure!" Peggy leaned over the console and waved. "Isn't that so sweet of him, Jane? This will be the best lunch, ever."

Jane hit the switch and let the window close off her tormentor. Then she decided she'd just trapped herself with another one. Cord? Peggy? She guessed it didn't matter much any longer. The day was beyond redemption, so she might as well make the best of it.

"Okay, evil woman. You get your way. We'll have lunch with that man, but there'll be paybacks later. You can count on it." She reached for the door handle and flipped the lever.

Before she could push the door open, Peggy grabbed her arm and quipped, "Sure. Paybacks. Anytime." Then she pushed the button on the dash and opened her own door. She grinned. "Just don't forget the keys, honey."

And she was gone.

BY THE TIME JANE reached Cord's truck, Peggy had already claimed shotgun, leaving Jane to climb in on the driver's side, taking a seat next to him.

"Thanks again, Peggy Lynn," she fired off as she pushed up the armrest to make room. She brushed her friend's offer of gum away, only to feel Cord leaning over her. Frowning, she already had a sharp retort ready when she saw the seatbelt in his hand.

"Just to be safe. Right, ladies?" He leaned into her as he snapped the latch.

"Hey, thanks for the reminder." Peggy held hers out, unlatched, and began searching for the connecting end. "Safe is as safe does!" She was smiling like the Cheshire cat, as if she'd planned it all.

Jane knew better. She was never safe around Cord Rivera. Not forty years ago, not now, and not in a hundred years. And especially not in this truck with his leg pressed against hers and nowhere else to go.

Oh, she hated this.

"Where to?" Cord's rich, honey voice broke the silence.

"How about Grubstake Barbeque?" Peggy was *so*

cheerful and buoyant. "It's out off the highway."

"Sure. I know that place. The one that was under construction two years ago, right? I saw it yesterday coming in."

And you don't know where we're going? I bet. Jane fumed. Yet, she had to admit one thing. Cord was at least being sociable. He'd always been the strong, silent type. Incommunicado, her father had once suggested. Cord had told her that he had trouble sharing his feelings. She wondered what made her think of that. What would he say if he decided to actually talk to her? I screwed up? I abandoned you? I left you in the lurch, and I'm a dog for doing it?

Well, at least I can make you wish you'd treated me better, Cord Rivera. Look at my hair. It's as thick and beautiful as it was in high school. Even if it needed a little color every month to stay that way, something she rarely admitted even to herself. And her dress, fitted, deep lapis cotton. Peggy had adored it at the shop, telling her it matched her vivid sapphire eyes. She was glad she'd dressed up a bit more than she usually did for a lunch date. She hadn't let herself go, and this man would see what he'd missed all these years.

Let him suffer.

Suffer? She was the one suffering, sitting next to him. She felt herself grow hot again. Five weeks after graduation, and he had dumped her, just disappearing. Then he'd married someone else only weeks later. How could he have done that to her? It was a betrayal that could never be forgiven.

That's why she'd stayed away from this town so long. Cord Rivera and his betrayal had hurt too much anytime she returned to see her parents. She'd only given in when Bill retired. Her parents were gone by then, and the oil had come in on the family farm. Then there was Peggy, her dear friend Peggy, Wicked Witch of the West.

And now here she was sitting next to Cord.

Time will not heal this wound, Cord Rivera. I know what you're up to, and you, too, Peggy Lynn. Tarzan and Jane are long gone, and I'm not climbing that tree again. You can count on it!

Out of the corner of her eye, she could just see Cord's face. He had a grin on his lips, and that made her fume even more.

I hate you, Cord Rivera. I hate you, I hate you, I hate you.

Her heart told the story differently, as did her leg pressed against his. And she couldn't even reach to wipe the impending tears away, because then he would know. He mustn't know what he was doing to her.

He must never, never know.

— 2 —

CORD TOOK IN THE broad expanses of the nearly
new restaurant. The paint still smelled new. The dining area was surrounded with green-tinted glass, and
just at the edge of his hearing, the clatter of glass din-
nerware sparkled in the background.

The aroma of barbeque was like a velvet glove,
drawing him in.

Even so, he could barely focus on the restaurant,
the views from its windows, or the tantalizing odor of
slow-stewed, spicy meat. It was Jane that had him
preoccupied, well, perhaps not *Jane*, but what he
needed to say to Jane, and that meant Jane was the
center of his preoccupation.

Time. It was said that it healed all wounds. Not
his wounds. Not the scars that crisscrossed his heart,

leaving him sweating in bed at night, wishing he could go back forty years and rewrite what could never be rewritten.

He had seen Jane's eyes, the way she refused to look at him. Her words, spoken to Peggy, hadn't been so muted he couldn't hear. Even after all these years, he felt the shame of what had happened brush his ears with fire.

He had taken the only alternative open to him, and it hadn't been Jane.

Dear God, that week had ripped his heart from him. He would have cast his family aside, thrown his own reputation to the winds, just to have Jane at his side for the rest of his life.

However, it was Jane's reputation, too. Him? He'd take the heartache just to be near her. For Jane? For Jane, he'd give up anything, even his happiness.

That was exactly what he'd done: broken up with her, disappeared, and married a woman he hadn't loved.

All for Jane.

Now was his chance to undo all that, and Jane didn't want him here.

"Cord?" It was Peggy. "Everything okay?" She placed her hand on his arm.

"You know me." He laughed. "I'm always okay. Why do you ask? Oh, and I see the greeter is on his way. Are you ready to be seated? Jane?"

"No, you don't." Peggy pushed Jane the way of the greeter. "You go on, honey. Tarzan and I will be right there."

"Peg—" Jane began.

"No questions, sweetie. I said we'll be right there." She pushed on Jane's shoulder with a light laugh. "Go, now. Don't keep the nice boy waiting."

"Said the Wicked Witch." Jane's eyes flashed, but she turned and walked away, her hips swaying in an in-your-face manner.

"Whew, but she's a bobcat, just like always." Cord chuckled, but he felt it fade away. "She's not happy to see me. Are you sure I should have come?"

"Now, Cord Rivera, since when do you let others' opinions of you dictate what you do? You tell me that. You're going in there and have lunch with that woman, because you two need each other. You waffle now, and I'll pinch your ears so hard you'll beg for mercy." Her face told the truth of what she said with narrowed eyes and a tight mouth. "I'm not funning about this, either."

"Funning?" He could finally grin, and it was real.

"Oh, you!" She slapped him on the shoulder. "Git, you hound dog!" She pointed the way Jane and the greeter had gone.

"Okay, trail boss. Your arm, though. I need forti- fication." He held his out, waiting until she slipped hers inside before moving forward.

"So, what will Jane think?"

"About what?"

"You and me as a couple."

Cord laughed out loud. "She'll ring the wedding

bells, glad to get rid of me for good."

"No, not Jane. We need Tarzan and Jane back together again, just like old times."

"Are you blind, woman?"

"Blind? I see what I see, Cord, and I see you two back together."

"And I see a woman who couldn't bear to look at me. That's what a seeing person sees."

"Well, it's just lunch, and we can do this, can't we? Just talk to her. She needs to know where you've been all these years. You can do it." She patted his arm, before releasing him to walk at her side.

"So, there's the happy couple!" Jane was in a booth, and she patted the seat next to her. "Peggy, I saved you a seat, unless you want to sit next to your boyfriend." She didn't sound nice at all.

"Hm." Peggy paused with her hand on her chin, as if in doubt about whether to take up Jane's offer. "I don't think so, Jane. Those long legs of Cord's, he really needs the side with the most room, and that's next to you. So sorry." With a grin, she plopped in the seat across from Jane, sliding over, and placing her black shoulder strap bag so that the rest of the seat was taken.

"So, I'm—" Cord stood at the end, letting his voice drop off. His gut was sour. Age was what he blamed it on, not taking his acid reducer that morning, and he pushed aside his disappointment that Jane was so antagonistic. This was to have been a reunion, not an emotional wrestling match.

"There." Peggy pointed without hesitation. "Jane saved that spot for you."

"Well, you're here, just like Peggy wanted." Jane glared at her before turning to Cord. "So, if we must visit, you might as well tell me what's been going on for *forty* years. Wouldn't that be nice, Peggy, to know what's kept Cord Rivera away for *forty* years? Make it good, Cord, because I'm all ears."

"Hum-ho, you're as feisty as ever, I see. And good morning to you, too, Jane." He chuckled, willing himself to get over his trepidations. For forty years he'd wanted to sit next to this woman, to have the chance to talk to her again. Well, it was here, and it wasn't coming back to him if he didn't jump on the bronc and ride it till the bell. "Well, I got married—"

"He got married! How about that, Peggy? Cord Rivera got married during his forty-year hiatus. What do you think of that?" Jane pressed her mouth tight, her irritation flashing from her eyes. "Was that it? Forty years and only a marriage to show for it? I thought you'd do something with your life. Marriage! Pshaw! That's nothing. I've even done that."

"Jane, honey." Peggy grabbed her hand. It had been waving in the air, and she pulled it down to the tabletop. "Where are your Sunday manners? Let him say just two words. After all, I'm here, too, and he was my friend in high school, also. I wasn't exactly Cheetah. Well, maybe I was." She grinned. "But I was his friend, too. Now be quiet and listen."

"You're right. I'll try." Jane reached to wipe under one eye. "That was very rude of me. I apologize. I thought I had all this behind me."

It was their waiter that saved the moment. Before Jane could say anything more, he stepped up and passed out menus, one to Peggy and two to Cord. "Good morning. My name is Holden, and I'll be taking your order, today. Would you like to choose from our new weekday brunch menu? It's been such a success on the weekends, we're offering it daily."

"Brunch? Absolutely." Peggy rubbed her hands together in anticipation.

"The brunch menu is on the back. Coffee for everyone?"

"For everyone." Jane's voice still had an edge, and Peggy frowned at her.

"Decaf for me," Cord murmured, fighting a smile.

"Decaf, sir?"

"Yes. With milk." He'd always consumed it black in high school, but times had changed.

"Mine, too!" Peggy closed her menu. "Jane wants hers black, like her mood. Waffles, anyone?"

"Let me give you a bit. I'll get your coffee while you decide." Holden smiled and made as if to walk away. "Five minutes?"

"Not necessary. We're ready," Cord announced. "I'll have the brisket, and wings and waffles for everyone. Mine with blueberries, the sweet lady at my side wants bananas on hers, and you, Peggy, strawberries, still?"

"Strawberries? Absolutely!"

"Anything else?"

"Extra sugar. We need to sweeten someone up." That was Peggy, and she nodded knowingly toward Jane.

"No sugar. Just the coffee, barbeque, and waffles." Cord glanced at Jane. Fire and ice, just like always. Well, she had been more fire at the end, and he couldn't believe he'd lived without her for four decades. Now, here she was again, just like all those years ago, if only he could fix things.

"So, your family. Tell me everything. I have to know." Peggy had her elbows on the table, staring at Cord, as if mesmerized by his sudden waltz back onto the local scene. She winked. "Speak up, Tarzan."

"Drop the Tarzan, Peggy. Please."

"But why? That's who you are. To the two of us, anyway. Right, friend Jane? Me Cheetah, you Jane, and you Tarzan. Now, swing for us, Tarzan. Tell all." Her eyes twinkled.

"I married, like I said." At Jane's narrowed eyes, he held up a hand for her to be patient. "But I'm not married now."

"You dumped her, too?" Jane's comment was muttered, but it was very clear.

"No, not dumped, Jane. I'm a widower."

"Oh, Cord, you poor thing. How sad. Jane knows just how you feel, don't you, Jane. Jane's husband died, and she's been so down, *for three years*. Haven't you, Jane?"

"You can shut up, now, Peggy."

Cord was beginning to be amused. He laughed. "Let me handle this, Peg, please."

"Peg?" Jane spit the question.

"She's my friend, too, if you remember. You weren't the only friend I had in high school."

"Obviously. After all, you did get married. Go on."

"Coffee's here! Everyone smile!" Peggy moved the placards on the table aside to make room.

"Here you go. Black, decaf with milk, and decaf with milk. I'll have your barbeque and waffles out in a jiffy."

"You're so sweet, Holden. Don't forget the sugar. Despite what my friend here says, we do need it. Don't we, Jane, sweetheart? Oh, did I say sweetheart? Holden, did you know these two were sweethearts forty years ago? High school sweethearts. Think of that. How old are you, dear?"

"Seventeen, ma'am."

"Oh, that's so sweet! Do you have a squeeze, Holden?"

"A squeeze, ma'am?"

"A girlfriend," Cord growled, glaring at Peggy.

The boy beamed. "Sure. Autumn Dumas. She's on the track team."

"Well, don't ever dump her, Holden. That just causes hot water for everyone." Peggy nodded sagely.

"No, ma'am, I won't. Oh, your food's here. Let me get you set up."

Once he was gone, Peggy laughed. "I like that

boy. He reminds me of you back in the day, Cord. Polite, mannered, and one to stick by his girl. Now for the rest of the story. I'm all ears."

And all mouth, Cord thought, but he let that go. At least he could keep his mouth stuffed with food for a bit. He needed a break. The barbeque and waffles had arrived just in time.

"ONE DAUGHTER." CORD pushed his empty plate away. "Veronica. She's married, in Lubbock, with two children. Closer would be nice, but what can I do? They had to go where the jobs were, and they weren't here."

"One daughter. You sure about that?"

Jane had spoken into her cup of coffee, and Cord looked at her, with one eyebrow raised. He chuckled and let it go as nothing more than Jane's irritation with him, questioning everything he said.

"She and Don met at Tech, married the year after graduate school."

"Your wife, though. What happened with her?" Peggy reached her hand to his, although she didn't quite touch him.

"Shelly? Cancer."

"Oh! Breast?"

"Lung. Cigarettes. She couldn't let them go, even at the end. But that was five years ago."

"You haven't been around here, though." Jane plunged in with her comment, her voice surprisingly civil. "Bill and I, that's my husband, moved back five years ago, and I haven't seen you around."

"We were in Sweetwater for twenty-five years. We were on the ranch helping Mom and Dad, but after they were gone, the place held too many memories." *Me. You. Why I left. Driving by your parent's place, knowing I'd never see you again.* He left those unsaid, though. That was old water, tossed out long ago.

"So, Sweetwater." Jane looked as if she was interested. She smiled. "Just for interest's sake, you understand. I've been to Sweetwater a few times with my church group, and I had no idea you lived there."

"Well, I don't anymore. Sold the place about six months ago. Now I'm back at the ranch. Still working for Pipeline Fitters, Inc, just like in the old days. Some things never change."

"You never sold the ranch? Good for you." Jane sounded almost enthusiastic. "My family never did, either."

"You next, Jane." Peggy reached across the table and pushed on her friend's arm. "Cord's bled his past. Now's your turn."

"Now, I never said—"

"Please, Jane Lane. Forty years I don't see you, and I deserve just the bare bones."

"Forty years in the next town."

"Not anymore. Just talk to me. Please?"

"I liked you in high school, Cord Rivera. I really did. But this isn't high school, anymore. Forty years under any bridge changes people. I'm not the silly girl

I used to be. I'm not naïve any longer. Don't you think I am."

"Please?" *For me? For old times' sake?* If he could only break the ice just for this one meal, then he would at least have something to take with him, a memory he could cherish, one that would hopefully replace the hurt he'd heard in her voice all those years ago. What a fool he'd been to not even go to see her. Who breaks up with the best girl in the world over the phone? Only a stupid, idiotic fool!

"Oh, sheesh!" Jane made a sour face, then let it smooth. "Sure. Masters in interior design at UNT. Bill, my husband, was an industrial engineer. One stepson, Billy, still married, and two grandchildren. They lived in Plano until Bill died. Now they've moved closer. Ages? I haven't kept track, but all teens, and you know teens. Enough?"

"That's so dry, I could mop the floor with it. You can do better, Jane." Peggy winked. "Did you notice he called you Lane?" She snickered.

"Yes, I noticed," Jane retorted, "and he's heard enough."

"No, I haven't. Billy, what does he do for a living?" Just the sound of Jane's voice was enough for the moment. Anything to keep her talking.

"If I must. Architect. I bet you want to know where Bill and I lived before moving back to the ranch."

"Oh? You were somewhere else?" *I kept away for no reason. How sad.*

"Garland. That's Dallas, if you haven't heard of it."

"I know Garland." He looked away and smiled.

"Everyone's heard of Garland. Be real, Jane. Cord's not stupid."

I was forty years ago, he thought. Anyone would be stupid to let Jane Lane get away for forty years.

"Remember all those parties at the ranch? Three hundred years in one family, and the best ones were when you were there."

Jane laughed, her expression nicer, almost pleasant. "Sunday lunches. Your family really seemed to like me. They invited me every week."

"They did like you. Very much."

"Just not you, not at the end?"

"Ouch. I deserve that, I guess."

"Enough of that. How long are you staying, Cord?" Peggy's voice was bright and engaging.

"It all depends."

"On all your new oil wells?"

"Oil wells?" Jane looked hard at him. "Since when are you drilling oil wells on your land?"

"Well, I couldn't let your family take all the black gold."

"We needed the money, Cord. Your family has cash to spare. You'll destroy the ranch."

Was there concern there? Her tone gave him hope. However, before he could engage her on the topic, they were interrupted by a familiar voice.

"Well, hello, Peggy and Jane. How's lunch?"

Jane nodded and smiled.

Peggy answered, "We're fine, Calvin. And do you remember Tar . . . I mean, Cord Rivera?"

Calvin Harris smiled and extended his hand. "Why, of course, I do. I see your name on paperwork at the bank all the time, and I've even faxed a few documents to you lately. I was beginning to wonder if I'd ever get reacquainted with you. I'm glad you finally decided to do some business in person. As your banker, I'm happy to assist you on any transactions that need to be made. We like keeping everything local and family oriented at the bank here. The Rivera name is a highly respected one. We've always appreciated your family's business."

Cord stumbled to his feet, annoyed at the interruption. This was to have been all about reconnecting with Jane. However, he smiled as he shook Calvin's hand and said, "That's what I'm here to do all right, take care of business in person."

His eyes were on Jane, though. She was the business he hoped to take care of in person. She might think everything between them ended forty years ago, but he hoped not. If only she would reopen negotiations, they might be able to do business once again.

She had at least broken down and spoken to him. That was progress, of a sort. And for that, he let himself hope.

— 3 —

AT LEAST LUNCH was over, but Jane wasn't
amused. She was back in the center of the truck, and
Cord wasn't keeping his distance.

Peggy seemed oblivious.

"So, you'll be at the Round 'Em Up Inn, I guess."
She had her monstrous black purse in her lap, and she
smiled. "Round 'em up, cowboys! Yee-haw!" She
giggled.

Jane ignored her. However, as much as she tried
to put space between them, Cord took it up with those
long legs of his. And Peggy! Did she really need half
the seat? Good heavens!

It was Cord's mellow, throaty rumble that got her
attention.

"Is there another hotel?" He laughed, as he pulled

up to the Center, parking next to Jane's red Lexus.

"If you get bored, give me a call. Jane might be conveniently too busy—" Peggy jabbed Jane in the ribs with her elbow "—but I have lots of time on my hands. I'd love to go out to dinner with a tall, dark, and handsome man." She giggled again, ribbing Jane once more. "Did you hear that, Jane? TDH, just like you like 'em."

"Yes, Cord. Peggy's divorced, now. She has plenty of time to go out with you, unlike me, who still holds down a job." Jane could hear her bitterness in her words, and she tried to contain it, but it was useless sitting next to this man. He did a number on her, and she hated that she let him. She took it out on Peggy. "She doesn't have to worry about her kids bothering you. They live in Colorado and North Carolina. I don't think they could get any farther away, could they, *Peg*?" She never called her Peg, but she couldn't resist.

"And I love it that way. It makes it so much more exciting when they come to visit, because they miss me so much. And," she reached across Jane and put her hand on Cord's arm, "they can't just drop off the grandkids like Jane's stepson does." She nudged Jane again.

"Oh, get out, Peggy. I need to get home." Jane was finally fed up. She could see Peggy's agenda, and she was having none of it. "Thank you, Cord, for the ride, but I have dinner to prepare. I have company coming tonight." She would now, if she hadn't before. She'd beg Billy to bring the grandkids over, even if she had to keep them all night. He and Jasmine would love that, to have a night free from the little tornadoes.

"Oh, Jane is a fabulous cook. Cord, we've got to get you out there before you get away. You cannot miss her fajitas. They're to die for!"

Cord laughed. "To die for, huh? I don't think I can afford to miss that. But I'm going to be busy the next few weeks getting the old home place livable again."

"See, Peggy? Cord doesn't need my cooking. Now, will you get out?" Jane felt her patience growing thin, although she was perceptive enough to know it was more than that. It was her need to get out of this man's truck. He had hurt her too badly to want to be this close to him for this long. Especially with what he was doing to her. She wouldn't fall in love with this man a second time, not after what he did the first.

He wasn't to be trusted.

"Not so fast, sweetie." Peggy patted Jane's knee. "Did I hear you right, Cord? You're remodeling your parents' place? Why, it's been empty for a quarter century. You must need the whole place reworked."

"It's not that bad. Dated, maybe, but no water damage, and the plumbing still works. Paint, carpet, and a bit of furniture. It's the hardwoods that need the most work. Refinishing's a mess, and I've put it off as long as I can. I can't move in until that's done."

"Well," and Peggy leaned back in her seat to open her purse. "I happen to have one of Jane's business cards with me. She does exactly what you need. It's only part time now, because she cooks all the time, but she worked for the biggest design firm in Dallas. The Ratcliff Company. Everyone's heard of them. Here." She held out the card.

"Jane, do you want me to take it?" Cord looked at Jane, then at the card Peggy held. "I could use the help. You have the contacts. I have to call every number in the book, just hoping to get someone responsible."

"I'm not designing your house, Cord." Jane took a deep breath. She wanted to get away, and Peggy was determined to smash them together. She wanted to grind her teeth, but her dentist would give her an earful, if she did. "Numbers, only. I'll give you those, but I won't be responsible for who you call or what they do."

"She's teasing you, Cord. Playing hard to get. She designs interiors for Billy all the time. She adores it, and the results are fabulous. She even did her stepson's office. Hubba, hubba! It's that amazing!"

"Jane?" Cord still hadn't taken the card. "Do I dare? Or would you rather me make my own decisions. Purple and green are my colors of the moment. And I'm considering an orange ceiling. Sort of that citricy, summer thing that's so popular now."

Peggy giggled.

"Orange is not popular and has never been." Jane

narrowed her eyes, daring him to tell her otherwise.

"Not since 1972." Peggy hooted. "I remember your bedroom carpet back in high school, Jane. Shag. Orange shag."

"That needed replaced, and my parents didn't have the money."

"So, do I get orange shag, or will you help?" Cord held his hand towards the card, but not close enough to take it.

"Yeah, Jane. Will you help?" Peggy moved the card closer.

"Oh, do it! Take the card!" Jane couldn't stand any more. She felt her eyes burn, and if she didn't get out of this truck, she knew she might not be able to keep her tears under control much longer. "Now, can I get out?"

"Almost, sweetie. Now, about an appointment. Cord, what's a good time for Jane to meet with you?"

"Meet?" Jane could hear the ragged edge in her voice. "I said I'd give him numbers."

"Numbers? They might paint his ceiling orange, and your name would be all over it. Is that the reputation you want? No, way, Jose. Now, I happen to know that Jane is free tomorrow, Cord."

"I am not! We have breakfast plans. We're heading to the Galleria tomorrow, and it will take all day." There. Dodged that bullet. Jane was relieved.

"No, girl." Peggy smiled wickedly. "That's how I know you're free. I've cancelled our day in favor of Cord's ceiling. It simply cannot be orange. Even you have to admit that." She chuckled.

"Not orange, and is tomorrow alright? For the sake of my ceiling, if not for me?" Cord seemed amused, but he also seemed to be at least trying to control his laughter. "I'll pay, whatever you charge, plus travel, lunch, anything. Whatever it takes for you to say yes."

Peggy was making no such effort at self-control.

"Take it while you can get it. An offer like this comes along only once every forty years."

"Sure." Jane had no doubt her sour answer sounded perfectly horrendous. However, whatever it took to get out of this truck. "You don't know my prices, though. I don't work cheap."

"She's not cheap, Cord." Peggy had her hand over her mouth, but it wasn't to hide her words, clearly.

"No, I'm not!" Jane had reached the end of her patience. Really, this time. "I do good work, and I charge a fair price. If you want a painter, they're a dime a dozen at 1-800-PAINTER—"

"I don't want a painter, Jane."

"Good. Who do you already have working on this?" It was her professionalism kicking in, she knew, and she didn't want this job, but good lands! She had loved that old house when she was there all those years ago. She could not let it be painted orange and purple. She would not!

"Well, no one, really. I had a cleaning crew in . . ."

"Good. I'm redoing that house. Top to bottom. I

trust you have a lot of money, Tarzan Rivera. You may need those oil wells by the time I'm finished. Now, out, Peggy!" She groaned as she realized she'd called him Tarzan, and was equally relieved to see her friend reach to the door and release the catch.

"Eight? At the house?" Cord sounded hopeful, as if he couldn't believe she had actually agreed to this. "Should I pick you up at your place?"

"I can drive, Cord Rivera. Unless you've let the drive go to ruts and rocks, and if you have, I'm redoing that, too. For a fee, of course." She pushed on Peggy's shoulder. "Out!"

The two women didn't say another word until Cord's Escalade was gone, then Peggy ventured, "Mad at me?"

"I don't know, yet. Maybe." Jane hit the remote, the car beeped, and she pulled her door open. "I ought to be."

"Saving the old house from a seventies' vibe. That's worth something, isn't it?"

"Something. This? I haven't decided." Jane was pleased that Peggy at least seemed contrite. She slipped into the car and watched as Peggy placed her purse in the back seat before climbing in beside her.

"I really am your friend, Jane. Can you trust me?"

"Can you leave my love life alone?"

"You're not a pretty widow. You need a man," said very softly, as if she wasn't sure how Jane would take it.

"But I am a widow. Can't you see that? You divorced Roger, and you've always thought, 'Good riddance.' I didn't divorce Bill. He died. Can you see the difference?" Jane felt her eyes welling up. She hated that Peggy had brought her to this, and after those awful nightmares last night.

"I can see the difference, but three years is long enough for any widow. You're too sweet, kind, and beautiful to turn old on me now."

"Oh, you're so kind." She thought the tears really would come, and she fought them. "No, I'm not mad at you. I just don't need Cord back in my life. You don't know what he did all those years ago. You don't know at all."

"I would if you'd tell me. I am your best friend, after all."

Jane started the car. She waited for a moment, as all the electronics cycled on. Brushing her fingers under her eyes, she let out a deeply held breath, then she began to laugh.

"What's that about?" Peggy adjusted her air vent and reached to the radio, but didn't power it up.

"Oh, nothing. It's that man. You think we belong together, and I know we belong as far away from each other as we can get. At least I'll get something out of him this time. Lots and lots of money. He owes me big time, and I'll see that he pays."

She was surprised that Peggy didn't reply. Instead, she pushed the power button on the radio, and she began to bee-bop with the music. Jane was pleased to hear her favorite oldie still playing. *Stop in the Name of Love*. Then she remembered and laughed to herself. It was on the car's hard drive. Of course, it was still on. Why wouldn't it be? Just because the song had been turned off didn't mean it had disappeared. It was there waiting on her the whole time she was gone, ready to start right back up where it left off.

Like love, but she dared not think of that. No, love was very different. Love didn't wait around for a repeat performance. When it was gone, it was gone, and it could never be replayed again.

She did hum along, though, singing the words softly when they came up, "Stop, in the name of love . . ."

— 4 —

"STOP, IN THE NAME of love . . ."

Jane turned her head to look at the face of her alarm clock. Six-thirty. At least her night had been dreamless. She turned her face into the pillow and let the song play itself out. It was her favorite, even if it meant nothing. Two men had abandoned her, one by running away, and the other by dying. She guessed it was all the same, though. They were gone.

"Oh, drat it." She sat up. "Eight is too early for an old widow like me. I should have told Cord nine, or ten, or maybe next year. Then I could sleep in."

She wouldn't, though, and never had. It was track day at the local high school, and she had to be there and gone before the teenage groupies showed. She did smile at that. They weren't groupies, not like she'd been as a teenager, attending concerts with Peggy and their other on-and-off friends. Then, they hadn't been groupies, either. Just teenagers laughing and singing along with their favorite songs, like, "Stop, in the name of love . . ." She belted it out with the radio before laughing to herself. She'd never been able to carry a tune, not like The Supremes. Then, no one sang like The Supremes, not then, not now, and probably not ever.

Especially not Jane Waggoner. Jane Lane. Especially not Jane Lane.

She hadn't been called that in more decades than most people had been alive. She'd forgotten how it rhymed. "Jane Lane." She whispered the words to herself. She had loved to hear it called out in the high school hallways. *Jane Lane. Wait up!* Or on the practice field over the speaker system. *Jane Lane, first up, in the 100-yard dash.* She'd never make the hundred-yard dash now. They'd be carrying her away on a stretcher. She'd do good to get in her two-mile jog before the high school girls began to lap her on the track.

And she wouldn't get that done if she didn't get out of bed.

Yet, there was her daily devotional on the bedside table, and she picked it up. She didn't look at it last night. Shame on her. It was Cord. He'd caught her off guard with those long legs, and Peggy was right. She did like TDH, and that was Cord to a T. And a D and an H. She giggled, then felt silly, like a school girl.

"Well, I'm no school girl. They don't have to get their honey blonde tresses from a bottle. That's for sure."

She opened the devotional. It just fell open, and before she could turn it to the correct day, her eyes caught the words.

"Be kind to one another, tenderhearted, forgiving one another, as God in Christ forgave you."

Oh, Jesus. Not that scripture. Jane closed her eyes, her heart pounding. *I don't want to forgive Cord. I don't, Jesus, and for good reasons. You know why, too.*

She glanced back at the book, blinking away the moisture in her eyes. This couldn't be King James. It was "as God for Christ's sake" in the Bible she preferred.

There, Ephesians 4:32 from the ESV. No wonder. The English Standard never got it right. She put the slim book down, knowing full well what she was doing. She was attempting, with every excuse in the book, to discount God's hand in bringing that verse to her mind. *Kind . . . tenderhearted . . . forgiving . . . as God forgave you.* She wasn't any of those to Cord yesterday, and he hadn't snapped back even once, and he sure had the right. She would have deserved it, too.

Oh, well. Today was another chance to earn her wings. She would try. Hard. As God *for Christ's sake* forgave me. After all, she'd played half the fiddle all those years ago. Her nightmare wouldn't have happened, if she hadn't provided half the devil's ammunition.

She had her running shorts, tee, and track shoes on by then, and she looked in the mirror. No one looks good at six-forty in the morning, she tried to convince herself. Still, she grabbed her brush and gave her tresses a quick swipe before tackling her sunglasses. She'd need them by the time she got to the track, and they'd hide her bloodshot eyes. Twenty minutes on the track, and she'd look a mess, anyway. But then, who was there to care?

Keys and water bottle, and she was out the door. It was only five minutes, but the track was filling up by the time she arrived. Too many old people trying to hang on to their youth, and she was one of them. She laughed at herself. Better than being in a wheelchair. That was certain.

A few minutes stretching, and she put the crunch of the track underneath her soles. She enjoyed the repeated crunch, crunch, as she made her way around the giant oval. Eight trips around, then home and a shower. *Might be tight to get to the ranch. Might be tight to get to the ranch. See Cord. See Cord. Silly Cord. Silly Cord. Tar—.*

Jane shook her head. That was not a mental running pattern she wanted to keep up.

Jane Lane. Jane Lane. Jane Lane.

Nope, not that either.

"Good morning, Jane."

She almost tripped over her own feet. She stopped, panting, and watched a very familiar man jog past her. She barely got out a "Morning" before he was too far away to hear her.

Cord, on the high school track before seven? She did this almost every day, and he'd never been here before.

"Well, it's my track, too. I pay taxes, and I can run if I want to." She tightened her mouth, waving at several people who looked at her funny, and started up again. *Avoid Cord. Avoid Cord. Avoid Cord,* she chanted over and over. That was all she had to do, avoid him, and things would be fine. After all, the track had dozens of people on it. What was one more? Who cared if Cord ran, too? It was just a high school track.

By her eighth lap, she was expecting each person who came up behind her to be Cord, and that kept her running at her top speed. He never did, and as she came to a stop, stepping to her bag for her water bottle, she looked for him. Over by the field houses, yellow buses were offloading long-limbed boys and girls, the slender ones that went out for spring training on the track. A few were already coming out of the field houses in their bright purple shorts and shirts with the team mascot on it. The giant bear with the extended claws was as familiar to her as her own hairbrush, but there was no Cord to be seen. She must have frightened him off, after yesterday's escapade.

She laughed and finished off her water. He'd called her a wildcat. Even her church hadn't erased all her fire, although she controlled it better now. She'd be good when she met him at the ranch, show him how a good Southern Christian woman forgave and forgot.

Well, maybe not *forgot,* but you couldn't have everything. She sure hadn't had everything in her life. Cord didn't deserve everything, either. Not her, anyway, as if he really wanted her again. He'd been done with her forty years before, and now he just wanted his ranch done over on the cheap.

Ha! She laughed to herself as she climbed in her car. Good work is never cheap, Cord Rivera. Not from Jane Lane.

In the shower, she got hold of herself. How could she react so strongly to a man she hadn't seen in decades? She and Bill had been happy. Even the happiest of couples had dry spells, and maybe hers and Bill's had lasted longer than some, but they had loved each other, hadn't they?

She let the warm water wash the tears away. She and Cord wouldn't have had any dry spells, she was certain. She wouldn't have allowed it. She wouldn't have allowed him to leave her, either, if he'd tried to break up in person.

Where did your Christian go, Jane Lane?

That was when she caught herself, and she was able to laugh. Jane Lane. She'd been Waggoner for four decades, and here she was thinking of herself as seventeen again. Fool. You never get seventeen again, and she had a house to remodel.

A dry towel, oatmeal, orange juice and coffee,

and she was ready to face that man, she thought. If not ready, then braced with caffeine. Besides, she had her favorite oldies on the radio, and she'd belt them out all the way over, on key or not.

As she drove up, she glanced around. She didn't see anyone. It was when she opened the door that she heard her name.

"Jane, don't go to the front. I was being generous yesterday when I said it was in pretty good shape. The front door's out of whack. Sorry! Go around back."

She looked up to find him on the roof, pulling a broken terra cotta tile out. There were several new ones lying off to the side. Cord was shirtless and covered with sweat.

"I thought that run this morning would have done you in." She waved.

"Just a warm up, I'm afraid. I told you I couldn't get good workers. I've been doing most of it myself. You are indeed a sight for sore eyes, you and your remodeling contacts." He grinned as he waved back.

Walking around the house, she shook her head. How did a man his age stay so fit? He looked as good at nearly sixty as he had at seventeen. She wasn't here for that, though. Cord was a love 'em and leave 'em type of guy, as her own experience had taught her, and she was just here to earn a few dollars to pad her retirement account.

Indeed, her thoughts were already clicking. Winding sidewalk, large patio. She could already envision a beautiful water feature with wrought iron tables, chairs, and an outdoor kitchen off the main patio next to the family-size pool. It was there in her head like it was already finished.

She hoped Cord wanted to keep the original integrity of the Spanish architecture. That was what was coming together for her, with pictures of a hacienda-style revision that remained faithful to the heritage of the original structure.

It was when she stepped inside that she almost stumbled for the second time that morning. The dining room. Memories. Cord's family, the laughter, some of the happiest moments of her life.

Her family? She snorted. Her father, closet alcoholic. Mom? Beat down until she was a wounded cur. This place was the only family she knew that was real, that had cared about each other, that had made her want to really have a family of her own.

When she learned that Cord was married, that was the day she packed her bags and drove to Denton. UNT was her home from that point on, a dorm for two years, then that little apartment with Peggy. Peggy, her family after leaving her own family that had been little better than no family at all.

"Well, is it worth saving, or should I level it and start over?" Cord came through the door behind her, pulling a tee shirt over his head.

"Oh, no! Don't even think about tearing down this house. It has so much character!"

"That's what I was hoping you'd say."

Cord stepped past her, closer than she would have liked, close enough that she could smell his morning run and his time on the roof all over him. Her heart turned inside out. It was the same as before. High school, football, the smell of him when he threw his arms around her to celebrate a win. It was Cord, just how he was, and how could she have forgotten his smell?

"Strip it all out—"

"No, you don't, not with me as your designer."

"Whoa, Nellie." He laughed. "I should have prefaced that with, 'The last designer wanted to . . .' Sorry. My apologies. However, that tells me I picked the right person for the job."

"Picked?" He *picked* her? "I seem to recall it was by chance, and I volunteered, if you'll remember." She laughed. She did like Cord. That had never changed. If the unthinkable hadn't happened, they would have married forty years ago, and there would have been no Bill or Billy, or the two grandkids. And she would have a child of her own, all grown now. But that wasn't real, life had gone on, and they were where they were. And it wasn't together, and that's the way it was.

"Okay." He smiled at her, and he picked up a short piece of trim. "You volunteered, and I'm glad you did. This, though. I tried to pick out some trimwork at the local big box, but I don't think this is it."

"It certainly isn't." She took it from him. "Maybe this would look good in a fifties' ranch, but not in this place. Your grandfather built this, didn't he?" She let her eyes rove to the coffered ceiling with its boxed beam structure. The insides were done with painted tin panels, and she'd try to save what she could.

"After the tornado of thirty-two. That's nine-teen—"

"Well, it certainly wasn't eighteen thirty-two." She cut him off, laughing and placing her hand on his forearm. She felt the fire leap from his skin directly to hers, and she immediately got quiet.

"Are you sure you want to do that?" Cord looked at her hand, then into her face. "Yesterday you couldn't even look at me. Today you're holding my hand?" His eyes twinkled.

"I'm not holding your hand!" She yanked it away.

"You could have left it there. I didn't mind."

"Well, I minded." She took a deep breath, certain the temperature had gone up ten degrees. "Texas weather. Not even eight-thirty, and it's already hot in here."

"Not to me," Cord mumbled. "Must be something else heating you up."

"Don't start." Jane raised herself as erect as she could. "We have to get off on a professional footing if we're going to get you into this house. What do you envision for yourself?"

"Four bedrooms are useless. Knock them all out and give me a big master and one guest suite. Then outside, lots of living space, shaded of course, and maybe a hot tub."

"A spa, you mean." She had her tablet out by then, and she was tapping away at it.

"Hot tub." He said it like he wanted to get a rise out of her. "For two."

She looked up to see him wink, and she laughed to show him she wasn't taking the bait. "I brought a tape measure, and I'll be busy a while. Why don't you go off and do some roof-type stuff."

"Roof-type stuff?" He reached up and ran his fingers through his gray-speckled hair.

"You know what I mean. Anything not where I am. Out, cowboy."

It was close to noon and a tablet full of measurements and notations later that Jane's concentration was interrupted.

"Are you about ready for some lunch?"

Jane jumped at the sudden intrusion. "It's just you, Cord. I was focused on my work." She let out a little laugh, but she was certain her face was pale. That had startled her.

"Oh, I'm sorry. I didn't mean to frighten you. I just saw you standing there and thought you might be ready for a break."

"You're quite right. I do need a break. I'll tell you what, I'm heading into town for a bit, and I'll be back later this afternoon. Will the house still be available? I'll need back inside."

"My house is always open to you, Jane. You must know that."

"Grow up, Cord. I mean, will someone be here. I

don't have a key, and you've already said you're not living here. Obviously. It's a wreck, and there's no real furniture, not even a bed. But that's what I expected. If you'll be here, I'll see you at one. If not, leave a door open, and I'll lock up when I leave." She took a deep breath, and headed to the front door, leaving Cord looking at her wistfully.

She pretended not to notice. She didn't need wistfully. She needed cash, and lots of it.

— 5 —

JANE BREATHED A DEEP sigh of relief as the garage door went down. While her garage might not exactly be *town,* it was certainly *in town.* It had been years since she'd lived on the old home place and considered it country. It was more like the town had come to her, but certainly not like Cord's place, out among the sticks.

Of course, it was the drive to get there more than how far away it was.

She was placating her guilt, she knew, like putting a bandage on a broken arm. Or better, like trying to fix a broken heart with a happy face sticker.

Still. At least her garage door was closed, and she was safe. Now for some lunch, even if it was the leftover tuna from day before yesterday. It couldn't stink any more than what Peggy had dragged her into.

Cord! Like they said, men. Can't live with them and can't live without them. But, after forty years, she had a pretty good head start.

She barely had her things on the counter before the doorbell intruded.

"Not Cord! How'd he find me here?"

Jane felt a moment of panic—she refused to admit to hope—before she realized how he'd found her. Of course! That Escalade had a GPS navigation system! She yanked open the door, prepared to snap, only to find someone much more familiar.

"Peggy! Why didn't you call and tell me you were coming over? I might not have been here. I might have been working at Cord's place."

"Well, are you?" Peggy still had her finger on the buzzer, and she pushed it one more time. "I like the sound of a door bell, sort of like an old friend come to visit, from forty *years* ago. Thanks, sweetie, for inviting me in." She flounced past, leaving Jane holding the door.

"I was, I'll have you know."

"You was what?" Peggy turned and grinned.

"Not was. I were what. No, that's not correct, but you know better English than that, Peggy Lynn. Use it." Jane heard exasperation buzzing at the edge of her voice.

"I know, but you said was, so I said was, and you never answered my question. You was what?"

"Oh, you!" Jane threw up her hands. "I was at

Cord's for the morning. I'm headed back at one."

"Oh!" Peggy dropped onto the sofa. "You were there all morning, and you're heading back. Here, girl. Tell me all about it." She patted the seat next to her, a wide-eyed look on her face.

"There's no tell about it. I was measuring rooms the entire time. Cord and I hardly talked."

"But, you said you're heading back. Was he here for lunch?" She peered toward the kitchen, as if she might see him there.

"What's with you?" Jane disappeared into the kitchen, calling back, "I've got to go, or I'll be late. What did you need?"

"Need? Everything!" Peggy followed her. "Have you even checked the mail this morning?"

"You do it for me. I'm headed to Cord's."

"To Cord's, or to Cord?"

"Stop it, Peggy. If there's a romantic side to this, it's between the two of you. After all, he already calls you Peg. No telling what you call him. Boyfriend?" Jane laughed sharply. "He won't even be there this afternoon, and he was on the roof all morning. This is a business deal, and I have a proposal to prepare."

"Then I'll just tell you what I got in the mail. It's our fortieth."

"Fortieth what?" Jane grabbed her keys and flipped open the door to the alarm system. "I'm headed out. Are you in or out? Stay if you want, but turn the alarm off if you need to open a door."

"Jane!" Peggy pulled her arm away. "You're doing this to irk me, and I'm starting to get it. Irked, that is. Reunion. It's been ten years."

"That's right! The twins, wasn't it? Skiing accident?" Their thirty-fifth reunion had collapsed out from under them at the last minute. There were lots of complaints, but no one had volunteered to step in and flesh out the details. Poof! Opportunity gone!

"Don't start. Speedboat, except they were fishing and got in the way. Kenny still has that limp. I feel sorry for him every time I see him."

"And Raymond still drinks too much. That's why I don't feel much sympathy. Bill said their boat was full of beer cans."

"Well, anyway, no one felt like hosting number thirty-five that year. So, we have to go this year."

"Says who?"

"Oh, Jane. Why do you have to be so grouchy today, of all days? What happened to my Christian friend who's polite to everyone?"

"Yesterday happened," Jane snapped back. "Oh, I should be sweeter. But I can't, not just now. My nerves. You know. They're not what they used to be."

"They're working pretty well today." Peggy pulled out a chair and made herself at home at the kitchen table, pulling a mini chocolate bar from a bowl piled full and unwrapping it. "I mean, I came here with good news, and all for you, and you cut me off like mold on a brick of cheese."

"You came here like Agnes and Francis came to church that Sunday, requesting prayer for their husbands, when they wouldn't have needed to had they been in church."

"I understand. This is about the Cord thing yesterday. You're mad, aren't you?"

"A little irritated."

"Too irritated to go to the reunion?" Peggy smiled sweetly.

"Did you notice yesterday, but you finagled me into a remodel job out at Cord's place, and I still haven't prepared my proposal? I'm pretty busy for the next few weeks."

"Surely you'll be through in six. You think?"

"Let me get out my crystal ball. Hm. Nope, can't tell. Sorry."

"Ooh! I hope you don't bring this snappy attitude to church on Sunday. We might need to pray you to the altar and back again." Peggy licked her fingers and smiled. "Really!"

"I absolutely need to go." Jane checked her watch, pausing for a minute. No one would be there to check her time, and besides, she wasn't getting paid just yet. What did it matter? She sighed and gave in. "Cord's not there this afternoon, so I guess you can requisition my time for a few. What's so important about six weeks? There are only about thirty of us left. You tell me when and where, and I'm sure I can make the time. I won't plan it, but I'll make a point to be there. Grubstake again this year? Everyone loves barbeque."

"Not Grubstake." Peggy had a bit of a coquettish look in her eyes. "Better, but you want to sit down for this one." She reached to her side and pulled out the chair next to her.

"Okay." Jane lowered herself into it, setting her clutch and keys on the table. "But not here. I'm not having thirty people in my house. No way. It's not happening."

"Better. Guess." Peggy grinned expectantly.

"Better, you tell." Jane glanced at her watch again and stood up. She wasn't playing this game any longer. She had to stop and pick up something to eat, now that Peggy had stolen her tuna time from her. She was surprised when her friend pulled her back down again.

"Rancho de—" She motioned with her hand. "Rancho de— Say it, Jane."

"Rancho de. I don't get it, and I've really got to go. Eat all the chocolate, Peggy, because I'm not. That's from Halloween."

"Yech!" She pushed the bowl away. "I guess I'll have to tell you, because it's only fair that you know. Rivera." She nodded smugly.

"Rivera? Is that all? Rivera what?"

"Oh, good heavens!" Peggy stood and put her wrist on Jane's forehead. "I knew it! A fever! Come on, Jane! Rancho de Rivera. I thought you should know, since you never check your mail anymore."

"Rancho de Rivera? Cord's place? It's a wreck!"

"It won't be in six weeks, will it? Well, I've told you my news, and I'm off now. You can get back to your little rendezvous with Mr. Cord de Rivera." She said his name with a romantic lilt and a grin.

"I—" Jane sat down again. "I'm supposed to get that place ready for a class reunion in six weeks? Have you been out there?"

"Once or twice. Here. I brought you my invitation, just in case you didn't have yours handy." Peggy pulled it out and laid it on the table. Opening it, she pointed, and right there was a map to Cord's ranch.

"He planned this? Without asking me?" Jane was irritated now, and she felt duped. Tricked. Again, like forty years ago. "I think I might have a thing or two to say about this."

"Jane, honey." Peggy drummed her fingers on the table to get her attention. "Didn't you say he was on the roof?"

"Yes." Roof? Who cared about the roof?

"I think he thought he could do it all himself. You know, throw up some paint, put in a few flowers. You know men, all git 'er done and no sense—"

"The no sense part, anyway."

"Yesterday was a lucky break for him, you showing up. Don't be mad at Cord. He didn't want to ask you. I had to beg him."

"You begged him?" Now this was a horse of a different color. "What does that mean?"

"Oh, look at the time. I do have to go. I have a class in fifteen minutes, and it'll take me ten to get to the Center. Can you take me, sweet Jane? My car won't be ready until later today." She smiled sweetly.

"Here." Jane pulled a set of keys from the drawer.

"You take Bill's old jeep. There's no air in it, but it'll get you there. I am not going to be late. The Center's on the opposite side of town, and I can't do both." She stopped dead. "Six weeks, you say?"

"Read and weep." Peggy swept up the invitation and held it out to her.

"Oh, but I do have to hurry. There's no electricity out there, and I must get all the measurements tonight. I can't do this in six weeks. How could Cord do this to me?" She flew out the door.

"Want me to lock up?" Peggy called after her.

Her answer was the squeal of the Lexus' tires on the drive as it tore away into the midday sun.

PEGGY PULLED OUT HER phone and dialed in a number. When it picked up, she laughed.

"Cord, you may have a wildcat on your hands. She's on her way out, and I can't tell if she's mad, glad, or sad. You know how hard she is to read. I showed her the invitation, so at least she knows what she's up against."

She reached back into the candy bowl, as she listened for a minute, smiling one moment and pursing her lips the next. Then she laughed.

"I know you don't deserve her, walking away all those years ago, but you paid your dues. Shelly was a jealous screamer, and I don't know how you stuck by her all these years. This is your second chance. Don't mess it up."

There were a few more minutes of conversation,

— 54 —

then Peggy nodded and said, "Good luck, Cord," and hung up. It was the last thing she heard over the line that pleased her most. She didn't know how fast Jane had driven, but there was a screech of tires, and she'd heard Jane call out, "Thank goodness you're here, Cord. I talked with Peggy, and we have a lot less time than I realized."

It was the word "we" that impressed her most. Jane was thinking of her and Cord as a team. If they could be a team for six weeks, who knew but what they might be a team for a lifetime, even if it took manipulating Jane into accepting what was best for her.

Anything for Tarzan and Jane.

And Cheetah, too, of course. Tarzan and Jane had to have a Cheetah, and Peggy would enjoy playing the part again, even if the last time she donned that suit was forty years ago.

— 6 —

"TOMORROW. WE START tomorrow and no later, no matter how many strings I have to pull."

Jane said the words aloud into the emptiness of the old home. She had the house to herself. Cord had needed to run some errands.

The timeline would be tight, especially as the sun was fading fast, and she had more work to do. There was no electricity in the old place, and the interior was growing too dim to be safe.

Still, all wasn't lost. She had her plans roughed in. She could come up with the details as the initial stages progressed. It was the rough work that needed to happen tomorrow, walls ripped out, electrical and plumbing started. Oh, this was going to be a mess, even if she already felt the adrenalin surge of the upcoming challenge as a tidal wave sweeping her forward with it. A good remodel was always this way with her. The challenge was the taste of life.

Heading out the back door, she encountered a more immediate problem. Her shoe caught in the doorway's half-rotted sill. As she went down, her first thought was for her tablet and all the information she'd loaded during the day. It couldn't be lost! She reached for it, and two strong arms got in her way.

"Jane, are you okay? I'm sorry I didn't get back from town sooner. It's too dark for you to be walking in the house alone!"

"Oh, it's you, Cord!" She was startled, and on several levels. She had been alone all afternoon. She hadn't expected anyone to be around for the rest of the day. Then, that someone was Cord. The real culprit, she pushed aside, was his arms around her. How had she forgotten this, how good they felt? "I, I think I'm okay now."

"Are you sure?"

"I said so." She *would* say that, even if she wasn't. "You can let me go anytime."

"You're right, I could. But what would be the fun in that?" He chuckled, and the deep sound rumbled in the darkness, complementing the night voices just starting to build outside. "Here's your tablet, although I think it might be too much for you to carry in your condition. I might have to transport you to your car. Better yet, to my truck. I think there's the distinct possibility that you might need to go to the emergency room, perhaps with home care afterwards. I'm very good at home care."

"I'm sure you are, but this has gone far enough. I think everything is in working order," she said, embarrassed by his attentions. "In fact, if you'll let me stand, I can assure you that everything's fine. And thank you for helping me rescue my tablet. I want to go over these plans for the house so we can get started on them tomorrow. Do you want to come by later this evening or look at them in the morning?"

"What's best for you?" He still hadn't released her.

"Turn me loose, Cord Rivera." She pulled away and fought to a standing position. "I'm not infirm. Remember, this is a professional endeavor. You lost any hold you had on me four decades ago. No touching. Back to business. Tonight or tomorrow? I also have to get a contract signed."

"Jane! How can you think that? You don't need a contract with me." He looked hurt.

"Oh, yes, I do. S.O.P. Every time." *Especially with you*, she thought. *If I'd gotten a contract forty years ago, you wouldn't have run off and left me. It would have been called a marriage contract, and I would have held you to it, buster.*

"S.O.P?"

"Standard operating procedure. Get a contract or get stiffed. Are you planning on stiffing me?" *Again?* "And I need to put in orders now for everything, and I mean everything. You don't know, Cord. Six weeks is an impossible schedule for a total renovation like this."

"But you can do it, right? It will get done?"

"Are you paying me forty grand?" She let that sink in. She hadn't really discussed money with him yet, but her commission would be at least that, if her figures today held true.

"Forty *thousand*?" He looked pleased. "To redo the entire house?"

"Grow up, Cord." She reached her stylus to tap him on the chest, only belatedly remembering how she used to do that in high school when they met between classes. "That's just my commission. Twenty percent plus reimbursable expenses. Like my gas out here twice today. And lunch, since this is a working day. It could easily hit another ten on top of the forty. I'm good, and I'm going to do it right. You do want it done right, correct?"

"Ouch. I had no idea. Forty thousand is twenty percent." He looked like he was doing some quick numbers in his head. "Yeah, I can put that together in six weeks. Sure. You got it. Where's the dotted line?"

She laughed. "You haven't even seen my proposal yet."

"You just told me, and I accept." He nodded at her, as if that settled it.

"Plans, colors, designs? Don't you want to see what shade of orange I'm painting the ceiling?"

He laughed. "Any color is fine, as long as you're the one doing the painting."

"Okay, then we need some clarification. I, personally, don't paint anything. My crews will do that. All I do is set them up and tell them the colors. And you're willing to accept anything I come up with?"

"Absolutely. Anything. I trust you implicitly."

"Okay. Done. I'll be on the phone tonight bribing all my crews to get them here on the double, tomorrow, if possible. However, I still need you to sign." She pulled out her tablet and clicked it on.

"You have a printer in that little toy?"

"I don't have to print. We live in an electronic world, Cord. Welcome to the twenty-first century. All I need is your signature on my tablet."

"Oh. Interesting."

She held it out. "Be sure to click the exclusion box, telling that you decline the right to consultation. That gives me the freedom to make any and all choices in the design process. This is a real boon to me. It cuts off days and days of haggling over minor details."

"Days and days, huh? What if I want to haggle?"

"Then don't click it, and don't expect this to be finished on time. I'm sure the reunion will go ahead just fine at Grubstake, and you can host the reunion for our forty-fifth." She smiled charmingly, daring him to push her even further.

"Okay, wildcat. You've got a pen?"

"I've got my stylus, or you can just use your finger. The tablet will resize your name to fit in the blank. Right there." She pointed, then took the tablet back when he was finished.

"We can still meet tonight, though?" He sounded hopeful.

"Whatever for?" She had the tablet back in her bag, and she looked outside. She would need a flashlight to her car, if she waited much longer. She was also aware her ankle had begun to ache. She hoped that didn't get any worse.

"I do want to see what you plan. You can do whatever. I don't mind, but I am interested."

"Well, I guess that would be okay. Time?" She looked at her watch.

"I have to meet with someone. Let me see." He thought for a moment. "Can I call you after I leave Peggy's?"

"Peggy's?" Now why did Peggy not share that with her?

"Oh, sorry. Peggy invited me to dinner. She said she makes great spaghetti and meatballs. I can call when we're about finished." He smiled. "She probably wouldn't mind if you came along."

"Sure. But I don't think so. I've had Peggy's meatballs. You'll enjoy them more." That irritated her, although she wasn't sure exactly why. After all, Cord wasn't hers, and he'd only been back in her life for two days. Six more weeks, and he'd be out again. C'est la vie.

"Then I'll just call?" He made it sound like a question. A hopeful question.

"I'll be at home. You have navigation in that

truck, I'm sure, and Peggy knows the address."

That gave her a good reason to exit without further ado. She did favor her ankle as she walked over the uneven terrain. In the car, she realized that her last five minutes at the ranch had almost been her undoing. Feeling Cord holding her had made emotions surface that she thought were long gone. How could she feel that way, when her mind knew how he'd treated her? He was the reason she'd been forced to live with the horrible decisions she'd made. Now, here he was like nothing had ever happened. She needed to be away from him. The farther the better.

In the shower, she let the hot water run down her leg and over her ankle. It was nothing that she couldn't handle. Still. The warmth felt good.

In the kitchen, she pulled a large salad out of the fridge and transferred a small amount to a manageable bowl. With a glass of lemonade, her tablet, and her salad, she made her way to the living room to organize her notes.

It was only when she put her feet up on the ottoman and rolled up her pant leg that she noticed the purple band around her ankle. And the size! No wonder her shoe had begun to hurt!

She hobbled to the kitchen—it was really hurting by then—and filled an icepack. On the way back, the doorbell rang. Pit stop, she thought, diverting to the door. She peered through, surprised at her visitor.

"Yes, Cord? I thought you planned to call." She opened the door wider, as she *had* promised to meet with him.

"Icepack, Jane?" His eyes fell to the pack in her hand. He leaned forward, his forehead crinkled with concern, and holding one hand on the doorframe, as though he would just step inside at the least welcome.

"Icepack. You're very perceptive. You didn't call." She shifted the icepack in her hand, in pain and now irritated.

"I did. You didn't answer." He made a face, a mix between a grimace and a smile. "I tried."

"But my phone . . ." She didn't know where her phone was.

"In your car, maybe?"

"I don't think so." She thought but couldn't remember using it at all since out at the ranch.

"Or maybe in my pocket." He pulled it out and held it to her. "It was on the porch after you left. I guess you dropped it. I would have missed it, too, except Peggy called to ask you to join us for spaghetti. Well, you couldn't exactly answer it, so I did. I told her you weren't answering your phone."

"Oh, you did, did you?" She looked back at her chair. Her foot had *really* started to pain her.

"What's wrong?"

"It's my ankle. I hurt it worse than I realized." She turned and limped toward her chair.

"Let's get you seated and your foot propped up." Cord helped himself inside, taking her by the arm, as she limped along.

Actually, it felt pretty good to have his helping

arm at her side. Bill had been rather distant most of the time, letting her manage her own aches and pains. She'd learned not to mention them at all. This? This was a welcome break.

"Does this hurt?" Cord gently touched the discolored skin around her ankle. "Here, and here?" He moved it slightly, causing her to wince.

"Only when you press on it." She laughed, but it wasn't funny. It really hurt.

"Point me to the kitchen. I need supplies." He stood, heading in the direction she pointed. After he disappeared, Jane heard him call, "Baggies?"

"In the cabinet next to the fridge, Tarzan." She winced, vowing never to use that name again.

"Found them," he yelled back to her. "Getting some ice." The refrigerator kicked on, the mechanism dispensing the ice loud even from across the house.

"I have an ice bag, Cord," she called to him.

"You need two." He stepped into the room. He looked around at the furnishings filling the space. "Pretty room, but you need to be in bed, and you don't need to be walking on that. Let me carry you." He put his bag of ice on the ottoman and bent to pick her up.

"No, you don't. I can stand." She did take his hand, and once she got on her feet, she proved she was right, but she knew that was as much as she could do. "Okay, I can't walk. Help me hop that way."

"I'll carry you that way." With no time for a response, he swept her up in his arms.

"Stop, Cord! You can't carry me! I'm too heavy. Put me down, now!"

"You're not any heavier than the sacks of feed I carry down for the cows on my place. What do you weigh now, a hundred and ten pounds?"

"Hundred and ten?" She laughed at his numbers. "I weigh more than that."

She had no choice but to point him in the direction of her bedroom, clinging to him as he carried her down the hall. She was surprised by the close guess, though. She only weighed about twenty pounds more.

Cord gently placed her on the bed and began to rearrange the pillows and pull the duvet and blankets back for her. She glanced around the room trying to judge the distance to her dresser where she had her nightgowns.

"What do you need?"

"Well, I normally do not sleep in jeans and a tee shirt. I usually wear a nightgown. I'll be okay, though."

"No, you won't, and I'm here to help. Tell me where they are, and I'll get one for you. There's no need for you to get up and put weight on that ankle. You can change while I go out to the truck and get my calculator. I still want to go over what I'm spending all my money on."

"If you insist. I'll need my things from the living room." She thought of her food. Well, wasn't this a mess? "I left my supper, too, a salad and a glass. Those too, please?" She smiled.

He nodded. "Gotcha covered, girl."

His remark was made in such an off-hand manner that Jane felt much easier immediately. She told Cord where her gowns were, directing him with her hand. He opened the drawer and pulled out a gown from the bottom layer. He then tossed it to her and headed out the bedroom door.

"I'll be back!" He called out, dropping his voice in a deep tone imitating Arnold Schwarzenegger, causing her to laugh and smile.

— 7 —

"OH, MY!" JANE SAT up and frowned at the lavender gown Cord had tossed her way. "This is entirely inappropriate."

It was one of her flimsier, short, see-through ones. Oh, well. She also had a sheet and duvet on her bed. She would be as protected from his eyes as she would be at a pool or in a sheer summer blouse.

Standing on one leg, with an eye on the door, she shimmied out of her jeans and tee. As quickly as she could muster on one leg, she pulled the gown over her head and threw the bedding back. There was no way she was having that man in her bedroom, with her wearing something like this. Gads! That was when her devotional from that morning caught her eye. *13 Weeks with Jesus.* How many weeks had she attended

First Congregational in the last forty years? And what had she learned from all those sermons? She sat on the edge of the bed and picked the slim volume up, remembering her verse from earlier. *Forgive. Forget.* How could she do that? She felt her eyes burn, and she refused to be red-eyed and emotional when Cord returned. He might think her an easy target—again!

She laughed at herself as she wiped at her eyes. This was a business meeting, for heaven's sakes. Cord wanted to show off his place at the reunion, and she had the skills to get it done in six weeks, if barely. It was no more than that, and she was a fool to think it was. She had about convinced herself that he'd returned after forty years, after a long and happy—she presumed—marriage, just to court her. And she wanted to hurt him like he'd hurt her. It was all so pointless. She was no more than a fool.

She flipped open the slim volume, praying, *Okay, God. Give me another word from you. Make it a good one.* She read:

"Be not hasty in thy spirit to be angry: for anger resteth in the bosom of fools."

Well, Ecclesiastes. What did I expect? At least it's good old KJV. But, no thanks, God. I don't like that one.

That verse hit entirely too close to home. She *had* been angry, and she *did* feel like a fool. But this couldn't be the random word God had for her. She flipped it to another page, certain that God would be kinder this time.

"There is no fear in love; but perfect love casteth out fear: because fear hath torment. He that feareth is not made perfect in love."

She slapped the book closed. She knew that verse without even looking. 1 John 4:18. Her Sunday school class had studied it just three weeks before.

I don't love him, God. Maybe once, but not after forty years. Do you remember what he did to me?

Do you remember what Mankind did to me?

Jane took a deep breath. She hadn't thought that, had she? What Mankind did to God? Yeah, she knew. And all about the forgiveness and all that. But this was her and Cord, and that had been a knife in her heart. She'd forced it under the rug, then Cord had returned, making the pain real again, just as hurtful as ever.

Just like when you are angry without listening to my word.

What word? She didn't want to know.

You're holding it.

She looked down at the book. *13 Weeks with Jesus.* What had she read today? *Forgive. Forget. Don't be angry. Love.*

What do you want from me, God? She felt the tears rising again. She wiped at her eyes, setting the book on the table. She looked up at the ceiling. *What, God? Please talk to me.*

I did. You didn't listen.

Okay. She calmed herself, taking a deep breath. *Once more and I'll pay attention this time.*

— 69 —

Forgive. Forget. Don't be angry. Love.

Oh.

She heard the front door, and she crawled under the covers, pulling the bedding to cover herself appropriately. *Sure, God,* she thought. *Well, here's your chance to prove yourself. I'll try to do my part, but I need you to do your part.*

And that is?

I don't know. Just do it, God. Please.

"Jane, are you decent?"

"Not for the past two days, but I am now." Cord wouldn't understand, but God would. "It's you I'm worried about, coming into a strange woman's bedroom." She laughed, making sure he could hear it.

"I see you still have your sense of humor. That's what first attracted me to you all those years ago. Jane Lane. Remember what people called you? Instead of June Bug, they teased you with Jane Bug."

"I'd forgotten all about that. Oh, what memories that brings up." She leaned her head back and closed her eyes. At least that could hide the redness. And she really had forgotten. Jane Bug. She had hated it then, but it was funny now.

"Your food. You said you had food in the living room, and I forgot. Where can I put this?" He held up his calculator. "And this?" He held up her bag with her tablet inside. "I recognized it from today. You said you needed your things, and I figured this was it."

"Thank you, Cord. On the bed will be fine. You'll

need a chair. Get the one from the make-up table in the bathroom."

"Right Bach!" It was his Arnold voice again, and he was gone.

"Better, God? I am trying."

The door bumped, and Cord walked in with both hands full. "Talking with someone?" He grinned as he set her glass on the bedside table.

"Just myself. You know, conversation with God, that sort of thing." She laughed and waved her hand at him to make it light.

"Had a few of those, myself. Let me get that chair, and we can get started."

She pulled out her tablet and tapped it on, entering her passcode to get inside. She tapped her way to the Rivera file, opening her Bridge program to allow her access to the banks of files she could use for inspiration. Rows of small icons opened, all ready for her to touch and drag into the Rivera file as key examples of the different features she imagined in each room. She began tapping them, dragging them to Cord's file. She knew them by heart, and this was the easy part. Tap and shift. Tap and shift.

"Whoa, there, Jane. Are you typing a letter?"

She looked up. "What do you mean?"

"Your fingers, ninety to nothing on that little glass thingy. What are you doing?"

"No. I'm sorry. This has all my idea sparkers. See?" She turned the tablet to him, and she touched the small icons one at a time. As she touched each one, a larger image exactly the same appeared at one side of the screen.

"Whoa. Hold that one." Cord grabbed her hand, forcing her finger back to one particular icon. The picture that pulled up showed a bank of French doors, all open, with billowing sheer fabric wafting into the room. "I like that. Can we do that?"

"I thought this was my project. You did sign that wavier."

"Oh. Sorry. Yeah, I did."

"But, yes, we can." She touched it again and sent it to his folder. "Now you have French doors and diaphanous fabric panels that will blow in the wind. How about that?" She sat back, smiling, strangely pleased with how the first five minutes had gone.

"Show me some more." He pulled the small chair from the bathroom up beside her bed. "This is fantastic. You click, and I have a house."

"Not exactly. There's still a lot of in between stages, like knocking out walls, and jackhammering floors, but, yes, I click, and you get a new house." She reached for a sip of her lemonade then pulled the bowl of salad to set it on the bed beside her. "Excuse me while I take a bite. I haven't eaten since lunch."

"That reminds me. Your ankle. How is it?"

"Hurting, but otherwise fine." She'd forgotten it for a minute, distracted by Cord's company. "I never did put my ice pack on it."

"We can resolve that." Cord reached to the foot of the bed and grabbed the bedding.

"What are you doing?" She wasn't dressed for him to take off the duvet.

"Get a grip, Jane. It's just the foot of the bed. I'm not going to ravish you or anything."

Absolutely right you're not! But before she could get those words out, she caught her devotional out of the corner of her eye.

Forgive. Forget.

"Don't be angry. Love. You forgot those," she muttered.

Cord glanced at her, a puzzled look on his face. "What did you say?"

Jane let out a deep breath. "Nothing. That's the end of that God conversation from earlier. Just ignore it." She chuckled. "*I'm* trying to, but God won't let me."

"It's just that I heard the word love, and I wasn't sure what you meant."

"I'm not sure, either. Now, about my foot, pull back the bedding. I'm in your capable hands." He looked at her strangely once more, but she just waved his look away. "To it, Dr. Rivera. Make the cripple whole. Wait, I think that was Jesus' job. Your job is to apply the ice pack in just the right spot."

"That, I can do."

It did seem to Jane that he held her calf in his hand a rather long time, much longer than it took to apply an ice pack, but then, she'd never sprained an ankle, and she'd never had a man apply an ice pack to one of her legs. Maybe that's the way it was supposed to happen, hold the leg while the ice pack does its work. Anyway, it felt very good, and she didn't mind him holding her leg. Not one bit.

— 8 —

"WELL, ENOUGH OF THAT." Cord sat back. He could feel the heat in his face. And on his torso and the back of his neck. "Let me get a towel to put under your leg so the bed stays dry." He stood and headed into the bathroom. He didn't care about the towel. He needed some space.

"Get the big one from under the sink," Jane called to him from the bedroom. "I never use them. Bath sheets, I think they're called."

He opened the cabinet. "Red?" They came in a rainbow of colors.

"No. ecru. The red might stain the sheets."

"Okay, missy," he muttered, pulling out the beige one. "I hope this is ecru."

He stood, pausing and refusing to look into the

mirror that spanned one whole wall. He knew what he was feeling, and it wasn't something he should be feeling in a bedroom with a woman who wasn't his wife. He should also go. That was the part he was struggling with. He should really go. If he looked in the mirror, he'd see it reflected back at him. But how, after forty years, could he just walk away? He was here. Now. In her house.

"God!" He didn't know if it was a prayer or despair. A little of both, probably.

"Cord? Did you find it?"

"I found it. Be right there." He did glance up, and he didn't see himself in the mirror. Instead, he could see Jane in her bedroom, sitting up in her bed. She had the bedding pulled away, and she was fanning herself. Maybe it wasn't just him that was hot. That was a relief.

Then he realized what she was fanning with. It was the bottom of her nightgown.

"Oh, Jesus, keep me strong."

"What is that Cord?"

"I've got the towel. I'm coming in." He kept his eyes from the mirror. "Ready, Jane?"

"Of course. Why wouldn't I be?"

She was covered demurely when he reentered the room. That was an onion shaved in a paper-thin slice!

"We can do this tomorrow." He stood beside the bed holding the towel.

"The bed will be already wet. Put it under my foot. Don't be silly." She pointed, pulling the mounded bedding out of the way.

"Oh. Sure. That. You're right." He grinned sheepishly.

"What were *you* talking about?"

"The house. It's late, and you're injured—"

"And better taken care of than I would be alone. Now, about that dining room ceiling—"

"No, really. I need to go. Anything. You do anything, and it's gravy. I'll love anything you do. Are you comfortable here for the night?"

"Cord? Why the change of plans? I thought you were interested."

"Ho, ho. You don't know." He chuckled, running one hand through his hair and turning away. "I'm interested, all right, and that's why I'm leaving. Surprise me. You always have, and I want this to be no exception."

"Sure, but I don't understand. Thanks for all your help." She set her tablet aside, waving to him as he stepped to the door. As he disappeared into the hallway, she called, "My phone. Cord, can you bring me my phone?"

He closed his eyes. *Give me strength, Jesus, If I go back in there, I may not make it back out.*

"Oh, never mind, Cord. It's here on my bed."

Thank you, Jesus. Cord knew he'd be okay if he could make it to the front door. The phone had made it convenient to just show up at Jane's door, but it had almost sunk his self-control. As he started his truck, he shivered at how close he'd come to making the same mistake he'd made all those years ago. All it took was being alone with Jane, and he was seventeen again.

Seventeen never comes back. Never.

He felt his hands shake as he pulled on the highway. He didn't blame it on his need for Jane. It was probably too much coffee or sleepless nights. Not Jane. Not Jane.

He must have said that to himself a hundred times before he pulled in the motel parking lot.

— 9 —

"JANE, HERE."

It was dark in the room, and the phone was cold to her touch. However, she was up.

Awake, anyway, even if not completely dressed.

Nightmares, or sweet dreams, depending on how she looked at them, had haunted her through the dark hours of the night. Years before she had dreamed of Cord, that he would return to rescue her, telling her that his phone call had been a mistake, and that he loved her as much as ever.

Then Bill had come along, and now she regularly dreamed of Bill's untimely death in the arms of that tree.

Last night, Bill hadn't come to her. Cord had returned to her dreams, but not the seventeen-year-old she remembered from high school. He had strolled into her night standing tall, with silver streaked hair, and, of all things, on her roof!

Now, where had that come from?

"Hey, girl! How's your ankle?" The words, bright and cheerful, so early in the morning, could only be Peggy.

"Better." Cord was still with her in her half-awake state, and she didn't have any banter to toss over the line.

"Well, that's a real conversation starter. What am I supposed to get from that? Like, is it still swollen, or, can you walk, or maybe, do you need to go to the emergency room? That would help me out."

"I'm sorry, Peggy. Did Cord talk to you? I don't mean to pry, but he must have. By the time he left, I was exhausted, and I fell asleep in my clothes." Well, that was the truth, part of it, anyway. She was in her clothes, even if it was her nightgown. And exhausted? That came from mulling over just why Cord exited so abruptly. After all, it had been his idea to come over in the first place.

"I get it. You don't want to ask for my help, and that's okay. I'll be right there. Tarzan made it sound like you needed an ambulance and an operation. I thought you'd be in a cast by now." She giggled. "He was so upset when he called me last night after he left you, that I could tell he felt bad about what happened. He feels like it's his fault. He sounded really guilty on the phone."

"That's ridiculous. I told him last night not to worry about it, that it was my fault."

"Sure, sure. Well, I'm bringing eggs and bacon, and you don't need to tell me about cholesterol and all that. Just for once, an egg won't kill your blood veins. So, get ready to eat up. And call Cord. He's worried about you."

"Sure. Kill me with kindness, if you must." Jane was sitting by then, and she stepped gingerly to the foot of the bed, tossing the damp, ecru towel through the bathroom door. "I'll be dressed and ready to kill."

"You do that, pumpkin." The line clicked and was dead.

"Well," Jane snorted, holding out the phone and looking at it. "Who claims to be the good Christian, now? Peggy, be careful, or you'll be taking first prize."

She did appreciate her friend's concern and phone call. And breakfast would be welcome. Her foot was part of the reason for her nightmares, she was sure, because it had throbbed, waking her up repeatedly during the night. It was only well after midnight that she had dozed off and remained asleep for any length of time.

By the time she had loose slacks and a cotton blouse on, one in complementary grays, the doorbell went crazy.

"Come on in, Peggy." To get there was too much effort on her shattered leg.

"I can't, sweetie! My arms are full. Can I get a

hand, here?"

"Oh, why do I bother with friends at all?" Jane groused as she stepped gingerly to the door. She swung it wide to see Peggy with a sack looped over each wrist.

"Surprise! Egg and bacon muffins on one arm, and nursing supplies on the other. One way or the other, you are going to feel better by the time I leave."

"I expected real eggs and bacon. Like the ones in a shell." Jane could smell it as Peggy walked by.

"It is. I didn't say I was going to cook. Gads! You do want to live to see another day, don't you?" She strode right into the kitchen, leaving Jane to follow. "Now, I want to see that foot, so don't wander too far off."

"Too far off? I can barely hobble."

"Jane the Hobblet?" Peggy stuck her head through the door and pointed, laughing. "About ready. You coming, or am I bringing it to you?"

"Here, please?" Jane found the ottoman and lowered herself. "I didn't realize walking would start the swelling again. I'll do better to keep off it as much as I can."

"That's what I told Cord." Peggy reappeared with a tray, orange juice in crystal goblets, and two red tapers burning merrily away. "Breakfast is served, and not too bad, if I do say so myself. You move to the chair, cause you're sitting on my table." She slid the tray onto the ottoman as Jane moved aside. "Oh, the rose. I forgot. Hang tight!" She flounced into the kitchen and returned with a long-stemmed red rosebud in a footed vase.

"Beautiful!" Jane reached for it and lifted it to her nose, drawing in the fragrance. "Where did you find this?"

"Um, that might be a sticky question. Because the answer is in your garden."

"What?" Jane frowned then let out a laugh. "Oh, you dropped the receipt. The name of the florist doesn't matter, because it's beautiful."

"No, no. I got the rose from your garden. You know that bush by the mailbox? It had that really tall bloom, and I just couldn't let it go to waste. I knew it would cheer you up, and that was so much better than wasting it out there."

"It wasn't exactly wasted. I enjoyed it every time I went to get the mail."

"Well, as I recall, you don't go get your mail, and so it was wasted. Now it's not. Besides, if you want to start checking your mail again, you've got another one about to open, so you won't even miss this one." Peggy reached for Jane's muffin and unwrapped it for her, placing it on her plate.

"I can unwrap my own muffin. It's my leg that hurts, not my hand."

"Okay, Miss Prissy. Then I'll take yours." Peggy swapped plates, reaching and taking a bite. "So good. I should have these for breakfast every day."

"And die an early death of clogged arteries."

"And die an early death, but a happy one. One day closer to Jesus." Peggy grinned.

"You're impossible." However, Jane had hers unwrapped by then, and she took a bite. "This is good. Very good."

"Told you." Peggy winked knowingly. "Did you call Cord?"

"I was getting dressed. Now I'm eating breakfast. Give me time."

"Well, he needs to hear from you. He's taking you getting hurt really hard."

"That's a laugh, him feeling bad that I got hurt." Jane rolled her eyes. "First, he came over, then disappeared as if I'd said something awkward to him. Second, it wasn't his fault." By then, she was irritated that Peggy kept insisting she call. Cord coming over was starting to feel a little self-serving, and that made her want to snipe at him. She murmured, "And third, Cord couldn't even begin to imagine how badly he hurt me."

"See? You're hurt, and you can't even own up to it."

"I'm not talking about last night."

"I get it now. You can't let loose of the past. Well, maybe it's because he knows he hurt you once and never wants to do it again. Have you thought about that?" Peggy bit into her muffin as if she'd something innocent like, hello, how are you?

Jane looked at her hard, thinking about Peggy and her pushy conversation. She compared Cord to the man she remembered from four decades earlier and the one who'd shown her such empathy last night. It seemed that he was two people. One was friendly and charming, and she loved that one. The other was careless of others' feelings, and that one had run over her with a steam roller.

Jane couldn't get past the steam roller. She bit off her words like snapping peas, and she spit them out one after another.

"He'd have to care to feel guilty, and since he doesn't seem to have feelings, I don't think he's capable of those emotions." Jane set her sandwich down and closed her eyes, leaning her head back. She didn't want to cry this morning, not after her dreams of Cord during the night. He'd been caring and concerned there. Not like in the real world.

"Now what?" Peggy tapped the side of Jane's glass with her fork. "The food's not good?"

"Whose side are you on, anyway?" Maybe if she had more sleep, or if her ankle stopped pounding, but that wasn't getting resolved this morning. Not with Peggy here.

"Quit it! You know I'm your best friend. All I'm saying is people do change over time. Maybe Cord has grown up some over the past forty years and is trying to let you know he's not the same person who left you back then." Peggy finished with a frustrated sigh. "Why are you making things so difficult?"

"Maybe if you knew the truth—"

Ding! Dong! The doorbell interrupted Jane's

crushed response.

"Oh, they're here!" Peggy jumped up and headed to the door.

"What?" Just when she was about to bare her soul. Maybe it was for the best.

"Oh, thank you. Flowers, Jane!" Peggy turned around with a huge basket of star lilies and roses with baby's breath and greenery throughout. There was a card attached.

"From?" They were beautiful, making her rose look forlorn by comparison. It had paraded so wonderfully before, standing alone and proud. Now it simply looked lonely. "Did you give the driver a tip?"

"Oh, honey, he said he was tipped on the other end." Peggy pulled out a card. "Here, who's it from?"

Jane took the card, looking at Peggy suspiciously. She expected it to say *Peggy* on the card. Either that or *Cord* in Peggy's handwriting.

Instead, it was a handwriting she remembered from back when life had been fun and easy, at least when she was at the Rivera ranch. *Cord Rivera,* with that little flourish at the end of his name that she always remembered. Now tears really came to her eyes.

"They're beautiful. They've already filled your house with love, er, I mean fragrance."

"Say anything you want, Peggy. Why didn't he think about how I felt all those years ago? I've grown up since that happened. Back then I felt so betrayed and alone. He didn't even have the decency to talk to me face to face. I never got to see his expression or let him see mine. He never saw my pain. Twisting my ankle is nothing compared to the heartbreak I suffered."

"Sweetie, sometimes you just have to forgive and forget, and start over from scratch. That is if you want to find love." Peggy patted her arm.

13 Weeks with Jesus. Forgive. Forget. Don't be angry. Love. Is that you talking, God?

"And unless you think I'm just blowing smoke, that's directly from God. Ephesians. I heard that on the radio on the way over." Peggy picked up her glass and tossed the rest of her orange juice back. "Now, let me look at that leg. I don't see how you walked in here, but it's not as bad as Cord said. I think you might even live."

"You think so?" Jane closed her eyes as Peggy began to feel of her leg. It was nice to be taken care of again, but it wasn't quite Cord. Not like last night. Had that been God talking to her again, or just Peggy? If Peggy, then God was getting desperate. She chuckled at the thought of Peggy with wings.

"What's so funny?"

"I was imagining you with wings. An angel, and I can't quite do it."

"Well, fancy that. I was just thinking the same thing about you. Daresay Cord doesn't have that problem."

"I bet he doesn't. Who's his angel? You?"

"Oh, girl!" She slapped the side of Jane's leg. "Grow up and step out of those Pampers. I'm talking about you."

"Ow, ow, ow!"

"What?"

"That was my sore leg!"

"Oh, honey, I'm so sorry!"

But as the tears rolled, Jane peeked, and from the look on Peggy's face, she didn't think so. And, oh, great goodness, she didn't know her leg could hurt so much.

She released her inhibitions, and she let the tears fall like rain.

— 10 —

JANE WIPED AT the tears.

Love. What's love? What she and Bill had? She had loved Bill, but she'd never been in love with him, not that butterflies-in-your-stomach, can't-wait-for-his-next-call kind of love, the one that makes a woman stay up all night, and the next day she's still not sleepy, because-her-heart-is-so-full-of-him kind of love.

She'd been in that sort of love once. Cord.

Somewhere along the line, about forty years ago, she'd broken his trust. Why else would he have left her, jilted and compromised, standing alone in her fog of grief?

Was she angry with him? Or was she angry at herself? She didn't know, anymore. She knew one thing. Her foot and Peggy's inept ministrations were bringing up muck that should have remained buried for all time.

"Peggy, can't you at least pretend to be gentle?"

"I am, honey. Well, as gentle as you need me to be. What do you think I am, the Easter bunny?" She snickered. "I do like pink, though. You know, they make pink elastic bandages. I wonder if they carry them at—"

"No, you don't, and I will not wear pink wrapped around my leg." Jane took a deep breath, feeling stronger, and she pushed the old desire for Cord into the dusty and dark corners of her memories. "I'm stronger than you think, little Miss Easter Bunny."

"What does that mean?" Peggy adjusted Jane's leg on the ottoman, and she stood, her hands on her hips.

"You know what I mean." Jane toyed with the rest of her muffin, debating taking a bite. Then she thought of all the miles she wouldn't be able to run, and she pushed it back.

"That you won't eat my breakfast gift, even if you're hungry?" Peggy picked it up and broke off the corner, popping it into her mouth. "Hm, yours is better than mine. I wonder how that is?"

"Justice?" Jane did take a drink. At least the juice was healthy for her.

"Now, I know you don't mean that." Peggy sat down, taking another bite, talking around the food as she was eating. "Tell me what's really got your goat, and I know it's not that foot. That foot hurts, but the pain's coming from here." She pointed with the last bite of the muffin to Jane's heart. "Don't you try to tell me otherwise, either."

"Got a coat hanger?" Peggy was determined to pull this from her, and besides, with her leg, Jane's endurance was wearing thin. She was about to fall through the ice, and giving in was her lifeline to sanity.

"You need a coat hanger, with everything else we're talking about?"

"You're about to hang me out to dry. I prefer to do it in private. I want in the drip-dry closet, not out on the clothes line for the entire world to see."

"So, you're ready to dish?" Peggy glowed in anticipation. "Give me the nutshell first, then we can go back and rehash all the details. I've been waiting forty years for this. Make it good, too."

"I don't have to make it anything. It's not like baking a cake, you know." Jane snorted in derision.

"Cakes are good." Peggy set her elbow on her knee and leaned in. "Icing on the outside, and all the tender tidbits inside. I'm giddy with anticipation."

"And anything forty years old is more fruitcake than devils' food. Trust me. I wish you'd left this dead. It's one of those things that only hurts when you poke it. You and Cord have poked it a lot the past few days."

"Whatever. Just tell me the story. Remember, bare bones the first time. I want it short and sweet." Peggy smiled encouragingly.

"Well, for better or worse, here goes . . ."

Despite the knot in Jane's stomach, it did feel good to bleed the misery and despair from that awful year to someone else's ears. She'd endured the torment of rejection, the pain of being alone, and the ridicule of her parents; and all with no one's shoulder to cry on. It had been truly a year she had wished gone from her life and memory, except that it never was.

Nothing, not time or marriage or a fulfilling job had been able to take away the worst thing that had ever taken place in her life.

"WELL." PEGGY SAT BACK, her eyes wide. "I knew there must be . . . I mean, I guess I suspected there was something deeper, just hiding under the surface. I never knew it was this big."

"I'm not the Loch Ness monster. Neither is my news."

"Pretty close, all hidden under the water, with just a tiny little bit sticking out." She looked at Jane. "Girl, I tell you what. You don't want to do the ranch house, I'll tell Cord myself. Buzz off, Buster!"

"That's not a solution, and you know it."

"I know something else. You're a stronger person than I ever knew. I cannot imagine what I'd do if a man ever did that to me."

"Divorce him." Jane smiled.

"That's right. I've been there and done that. Still, at eighteen? You were fighting this battle all alone while I was still hoping for my first real kiss, and no, those prom pecks on the cheek don't count."

"I was in love. Truly. I would have given Cord anything. For a long time after, I would have forgiven him, if he'd just let me know there was a reason for what he'd done."

"Truly? Oh, you *are* being generous. Like forgiving a rattler that's just bitten you."

"When you truly love someone, you don't care. I just couldn't maintain that forever." Jane took a deep breath as she looked away. "I had to move on. Bill offered me his life and his son, and I took him up on the offer. I'm not sorry, either, even if what we had was less than what I wanted."

"Been there, remember." Peggy patted Jane's shoulder. "Haven't wanted to go there again. Not just yet, anyway."

The jangling of the phone burst into the moment, and both women laughed.

"Yes, Jane Waggoner speaking." She looked at Peggy with a frown. "I have a what?" She covered the mouthpiece, whispering to Peggy. "Do you know anything about an appointment?"

"Hair or nail?" Peggy glanced at her fingers. "I have one that's peeling, so make one for me while you're at it." She put it to her mouth to chew the edge.

"It'll be brain surgery, then. It's Dr. Widdener," Jane teased. "The surgeon's office finally found you."

"Oh, so it's not hair or nail. He only does ordinary

stuff. Tell him I don't need anything."

"It's for me, not you." Jane spoke into the phone, "What's this for, if I may ask?"

Peggy stood, whispering, "I would expect a broken heart. Confirm it, Jane, then we'll get you back in hot pursuit for a new man." Peggy laughed, reaching for the plates. "You take care of your conversation, and I'll get things cleaned up."

Jane waved her hand at her, talking into the phone. "I don't have an appointment." She listened a minute more, then said, "10:40, it is. I'll be there. Thank you." That gave her less than an hour.

"So, what does *your* brain surgeon need?" Peggy called from the kitchen, and there was laughter in her voice.

"He was looking for you, remember?"

"But, and I will continue, even though you interrupted me, so why would he be calling you?"

"How come you can hear every word every single person whispers in Sunday school, but you can't hear the sarcasm in my voice? It's Dr. *Widdener*." Jane handed Peggy her glass. "Take this, too, since you're playing house maid."

"For all I know, Dr. Widdener could be a brain surgeon. Maybe there are two Dr. Widdeners in this town." But Peggy had a smile on her lips as she said it.

"It's my foot. Someone scheduled an X-ray."

"Good. You need one. Did I hear 10:40?"

"So you do listen." Jane smirked.

"Of course. I just choose what I want to forget. Who scheduled it?"

"They didn't say. I thought you."

"Guess again, and oh, look at the time." Peggy picked up Jane's keys from the table. "Are we taking your car? I'd look good driving your red Lexus."

"Right. Look at the time, and you have a class at ten. I drove home last night. I'm sure I can make it to the hospital."

Actually, she wasn't. If Peggy didn't schedule the appointment, it had to have been Cord. He was the only other one who knew, and she wasn't calling that man for a ride. She'd rather skip the appointment, even if it took another week to get in or she had to wait in the emergency room for twelve hours, before she asked Cord over here again.

"If you don't mind waiting afterwards, I can juggle you in." Peggy sat on the edge of the ottoman and placed her hands in her lap contritely, holding her keys in her hand, as she studied Jane's face.

"Juggle me in?" Juggling was the last thing she needed with her sore ankle.

"I'd just have to pick you up after class. Do you want to wait that long? If not, I can call Cord."

"No, you cannot call Cord. You head on. I can manage fine by myself."

"Suit your own manikin. When you're crippled for life, just tell the doctor that a very good friend offered you a ride, and you refused." Peggy stood with emphasis and opened the door. "Not too late to take me up on my offer."

"Out!"

It was after her awkward and actually quite diffi-cult shower that the phone rang again. The hospital, surely, telling her the appointment had been a mis-take. She hopped to answer it. "Hello?"

"It's me. Thought you might need a ride." Noth-ing else.

Cord! Here to be her knight in shining armor. Her eyes narrowed, but the tingle in her stomach told her she didn't mind. The pain in her ankle screamed a little louder. It cried, Thank you!

"Did you set this up?" It had to have been him.

"Set up what? I'm just the taxi service." His amusement bled through with his words.

"Doesn't matter. I'm glad you're here. Give me ten minutes."

He clicked off without replying, and Jane set the phone down. Now, she was under pressure. Ten minutes to be beautiful. She didn't know if she could do it.

A hint of makeup, quick mascara and too-heavy lipstick, and she headed for the closet. Black crops and slinky lavender fit the bill. Cord would be wowed. Then, one squirt of her favorite perfume, and she stood back to admire the damage as well as she could with one hobbled ankle and a time frame short-er than a high-speed raindrop filmed as it fell, splat-tering all over a windshield.

She felt about to splatter over a windshield. But

two people now knew the truth, and she had someone at her back she could call for an emergency survival rescue. At least she hoped Peggy was now on her side.

When she opened the door, there was Cord, not sitting in his truck, but waiting on the step. He held out his arm to take hers, and she was relieved. She might have had to ask for it, and she didn't want to make out that she needed him. She preferred for him to think she was just being polite by accepting.

It was better that way.

"I thought I knew beautiful, then you walked out the door." He said it looking straight ahead.

"Ha," she replied. "Let's get down and get your eyes checked." Secretly, his comment pleased her immensely. He sounded sincere, and while he hadn't exactly said she was beautiful, it was very close. She hadn't heard that from someone who meant it in a long time.

"I'm an eagle, and I sighted the best thing in the landscape."

She yanked his arm. "What does that mean?" But she laughed, too. Just like always, he drew her in with his charm. Away from him, she was safe. In his presence? No one was safe in the presence of Tres Juan.

"If only you could see through my eyes, my little senorita, you would know the most beautiful thing in the world is at my side."

"I know a charmer when I hear one. I'm coated with lead. You're not getting through that easily."

Yet, despite her words, she knew he'd made a big dent. She refused to check her plating too closely. He might have pierced it, and she didn't want to admit to that.

She did notice Cord smiling, and in that moment, she suspected he'd gotten just what he wanted. And she couldn't even hate him for it, because, as much as she hated to admit it, the tiniest part of her wanted it, too.

— 11 —

"WELL, THAT'S ENOUGH of waiting." Cord stood abruptly, stepping across the waiting room to lean against the counter. "Ma'am, when do you think the results will come in?"

"It will be a moment, sir. We'll call you when the X-rays are ready." The receptionist smiled, but she held her pen poised, a signal that she had clearly been interrupted.

It hadn't information that Cord needed. It was space from Jane. To sit next to her was to be a rocket attached to a jet airplane, buffeted constantly by unseen winds and the forces of nature.

"Thank you. Should I just wait over there?" He nodded his head towards the seat he'd just left.

"Probably. There's free coffee down the hall in

the cafeteria. Donuts, too, if there are any left. By this time, no promises." She smiled pleasantly, but it was clear he was being dismissed.

"Thank you." He turned away, catching Jane flipping disinterestedly through a magazine. She was beautiful, just as much so as he'd thought her in high school. What a fool he was! Still, water under the bridge and so on. What had been done couldn't be undone. He could only go on from here.

"Coffee?" He walked as close as he dared.

"Only if you make it black. No sugar needed." She didn't look up.

"Ouch." He remembered Peggy's remark in the restaurant. With sugar, to sweeten Jane's black mood.

"Why ouch?" Jane looked up, with just the hint of a smile on her lips. She set the magazine aside.

"Nothing. It's just that, yesterday . . ." He ran his fingers through his hair, leaving one spot mussed, the ends sticking out awkwardly. Then he hit it again, the hair lying flat the second time. "Well, black? Really?"

He wasn't sure he wanted to get into yesterday. Not and mess up what they had right then. After all, Jane was here, and he was here, and they were in the same room, even if it was the hospital for an injury she had received at his ranch.

Still. Here. Them. Together.

"Black, really. Sometimes we need to get rid of the sugar coating and deal with the real issues, don't you think?"

Oh, my, he thought. "Sugar coating?" He really

should go for the coffee and let this fade away into, perhaps, next year.

"Jane Waggoner?"

"Here." Jane held out her hand. "That's for us. Help me stand."

"Guess the coffee'll have to wait. After, maybe." Cord reached for her hand. It was warm and a little moist. Nervousness about the results of the X-ray, he figured.

"Maybe." She walked gingerly. "It's called follow-through."

"Follow-through?" A nurse was just in front of them, waiting. "What does that mean?"

"Keeping promises. Do you promise coffee, or only if it's convenient?"

"What?" He had no idea what that meant. It had been just coffee, and just to fill the time. Or, at least, to give him space to think clearly.

"Think, Cord, think." Jane stopped and tapped him on the forehead with her knuckles. "What have our lives been about? Yours and mine?"

He did notice her eyes were red, but then the nurse was there, and they were invited into a small consulting room.

"A bad sprain, Mrs. um, Rivera?" The unfamiliar doctor looked at a chart. "Ah, Mr. Rivera. I'm Dr. Perkins."

Jane laughed and coughed, covering her mouth with her hand. "Not Mrs. Rivera."

"No? My apologies. The notation is that Mr.

Rivera made the appointment and is paying the bill."
The doctor shrugged.

"Mrs. Waggoner is working for me. She was injured on the job." Cord felt himself warm. He held out his hand. "Cord Rivera. This is Jane Waggoner. It's nice to meet you, Dr. Perkins."

"Ah, I see. Waggoner." He marked on the chart, scratching something out and writing a note. "Let me pull up your X-rays on the screen." The doctor turned to a computer on a side table.

"So, I'm an employee? Do all your employees get coffee and an X-ray?" Jane whispered the words to Cord.

"Do you still want the coffee?" Cord sank lower in his chair. Employee? Why couldn't he have said friend? "With just a little sugar?"

"Now, what does that mean?"

The doctor interrupted. "Ah, now, here we see the damage." He went on to explain that it was no more than a bad sprain, but a bone density test might be advisable to guard against the possibilities of early-onset osteoporosis. "Elevation. That's the key. Keep the leg elevated and put heat and ice on it for a few days. It should heal just fine."

On the way out, Jane paused on the steps, and she touched Cord's arm.

"Yes?" He had his key in his hand and was just slipping his sunglasses on his face.

"My coffee?"

"Oh, I forgot." She was right. He wasn't dependable. Still, he could fix that. "There's Grubstake. I can get you a coffee there."

She laughed. "Not Grubstake. Let's try IHOP. It's easier to get in and out." She offered her arm again. "Oh, and thank you in there."

"For?" Just the feel of her arm energized him. "I didn't do anything except forget your coffee."

"You met the doctor with me. I appreciate that."

"Thank you, but what else would I have done? Sat and read a magazine?"

"Some people would." She brushed her hair from her face, only to have the wind catch it and blow it back over her chin.

"Fools. Only a fool would do that."

"Bill did." She looked away.

Cord didn't think she'd meant for him to hear, but he had. He wondered if that was a positive comparison or not. He glanced at his watch. "11:55. Do you think IHOP can serve lunch with that coffee?"

"Um . . ." She looked frightened; wary, as if lunch might be a dangerous assignation.

"No lunch?" Was that indecision he heard? He watched her face, seeing emotions flickering across its surface. "What is it, Jane?"

She brightened. "Why, thank you, Tarzan. I think that would be lovely. What restaurant did you have in mind?" She ended with her voice almost in a whisper, as if she'd made the effort to be bright and cheerful, but it had been difficult.

If only he could tell her everything had been a

mistake with Shelly, and if only she would believe him. More importantly, he could tell her about Veronica, his daughter. He wanted to set the record straight.

However, the way he felt at this moment, he just wanted Jane. The ache had never gone away, no matter what he'd done over the past forty years.

He knew that's why he'd been so successful in his job. The ache had driven him to fill up his life with something, and the oil fields had allowed him to do that. The work was hard, the hours long, and he hadn't had to think much of the time. It was easier to fall into bed exhausted and numb than to think about how he wished life had been.

Nevertheless, it was his fault, and he had owned up to that. Now, he had a chance to make things right with Jane. That was what he wanted most. He wanted her to trust him again, and then maybe, just maybe she would love him again, too.

He was determined to find a way, and get through to her, he would.

— 12 —

"DAIRY QUEEN! I THOUGHT I said IHOP." Jane laughed. She hadn't been here in twenty years, and it hadn't changed in forty, except perhaps the fresh paint and the newer, brighter marquee. "Cord, I had no idea this place was still in business."

"And how long did you say you've been back?" He chuckled as he turned into the lot. "Don't mind me. I'm not surprised you didn't know. It just reopened last month."

"No. It was closed? Why?" She knew she'd been in a fog since Bill's death, but to not know this? True, she didn't do the fast food thing much, not watching her waistline, but to have missed this entirely?

"It's a new building. See that empty lot across the street? That's where it used to be."

"Oh, get out of here." Jane found she was enjoying Cord's company, and she felt good for a change, like life was coming up before her, a brilliant sunrise in her soul. "This is the place I remember, except for that high-tech sign running the length of the building. Look at that! They still have banana splits, and they're on sale today. What I wouldn't give to be seventeen again!"

"That empty lot is what you remember. Peggy filled me in. There was an uproar about the place being a local landmark, but the new highway in the works preempted that, so they assuaged the naysayers with this retro building. It's all new and modern inside, with flush toilets and everything."

"I guess I should get out more." She felt an unwelcome tug on her heart, a reconnection with all those happy moments when she and Cord were really in love, she supposed. "Too bad all this got away from us."

"Did it?" The truck was still running, and Cord reached to the dash to cut the engine. "It's here. We're here. We can do this over again."

"That's a nice dream." A very nice dream, but one that had evaporated in fog and mist, burned away by the brutal sun of reality. This was just lunch. Coffee and perhaps a bite to eat. No more. It didn't have to be fog and mist, a reconstructed dream. It only had to be lunch. It might even be fun. "It's crowded."

"You'll be surprised. It's bigger on the inside than it looks from here." He reached for the door.

"Ready?"

She looked at him. Was that anticipation in his voice? His inflection was so familiar, a thing he'd done all those years ago when they went somewhere. Like he was excited to show her off, like he was proud of her, and he wanted the world to know. She missed that. She'd enjoyed it then, she'd lost it with Bill, and it felt good.

It was the abandonment that hadn't been so wonderful, and she couldn't risk that again. Not even for this. However, she could enjoy it for this one day. Then, she could climb back in her shell and be morose and grumpy about life mistreating her with Bill's death and, she grudgingly admitted, losing Cord all those years ago.

"What?" Cord still had his hand on the door.

She realized she'd been looking at him but hadn't answered. "Nothing. Just . . ." It was, too, something, but that was old water, and she wasn't sure the bridge was even still there.

"Look at that." He pointed. "That cannot be . . . but it is. That's Eddy Burns." He laughed. "And he's coming this way. He's still got those big teeth. Remember, Jane? Rodeo team? We nicknamed him after that horse from TV."

"Horse? What TV?" She searched for the memory. "From when we were kids?"

"You know. That show with the talking horse."

Jane remembered, and she felt the giggles well up in her. "Oh, *that* TV show. Mr. Ed, the talking horse

TV show."

"I think he's coming to talk to us." Cord grinned, reaching and placing a hand conspiratorially on hers. "Should I roll down the window or speed away, spinning my tires?"

"You cannot speed away, not if he's coming to see us." She didn't even notice the hand. It was as natural as being here with Cord in this truck. Instead, a picture of Eddy from school flashed into her head. He'd been skinny, and when he smiled, his teeth were the only thing you noticed. It would be hard not to call him Mr. Ed. It had been mean, but everyone had done it behind his back.

Cord put his finger on the window control. "No funny business, now." He looked at her and grinned.

"We can't laugh at him, Cord."

"That might not be feasible." Cord's eyes twinkled. "Here goes." He hit the window control, and it slipped soundlessly into the door. "Eddy." He reached his hand through the window.

"I thought that was you, here in this fancy truck. And there, Jane? Jane Waggoner? Fancy seeing you two together, and here." He glanced at the restaurant. "Just like old times, huh? Tarzan and Jane-bug. Y'all coming in?"

Jane tried to cover her mouth, but Eddy's teeth were all she could see. He carried more weight now, and walking over, he'd looked fine. As soon as he started to talk, it was high school all over, and she couldn't control herself. Laughter poured from her.

Cord looked at her, and he began to laugh, covering his eyes with his hand.

"What's so funny, Jane? You and Tarzan have some inside joke you want to share with me?"

"Nothing, nothing at all. We were just thinking about the good old days, that's all." Jane tried to speak without her voice bursting into a fit of giggles, but it was hard, and she knew she wasn't being successful. That brought on another set of giggles.

"Well, Tarzan, I haven't seen you around here in a while. Where you been keeping yourself?" Eddy's teeth continued to flash, causing a new round of laughter from inside the truck.

"Been busy, but now that retirement's looming, I thought I might move back to the hacienda. I'm having some renovation done, and Jane's helping me with the design work."

"That's right." Eddy's teeth flashed, his grin exposing white against his tanned skin. "The reunion. It's out there, isn't it? I'd wondered about that, you being gone and the place empty so many years. I noticed some big trucks out your way. You thinking of drilling?"

Jane watched the men talking, but it was the scar on Cord's cheek that had her attention. It was her fault, and the memory came back sharp and clear. Barbed wire. It was because of that fence he'd been repairing. She'd been at the ranch for the day, and his mother had asked her to carry the hands' lunch to them in the ranch's old Jeep. When he saw it was her getting out, he raised his hand to wave, the wire cutters held high, and a coil filled with razor sharp barbs had leaped to his face, leaving a bloody cut six inches long.

It was still visible after all these years, just barely, when he smiled, a part of her life that he carried with him every day. She wondered if he remembered that day, and when he saw it in the mirror, if it reminded him of her. She shook her head, taking a deep breath.

"Eddy?" She had to get out of this truck. She was sinking way too far into old memories that were entirely too, too, *something*. Enticing, if no other word fit.

"Yes?" He smiled at her, those big teeth coming through loud and clear.

"Cord and I were headed inside. What about you?"

"Yeah, Eddy. You had lunch? Jane and I, we were—"

"I couldn't intrude. You, too, now that you're back together—"

"No, Eddy. We're not back together." Jane interrupted, grabbing her door. "This is a working relationship, only." She released the latch, and she pushed the door wide. "Cord, I need help getting down, please. The doctor said not to put any pressure on this, and this truck is very tall."

She looked back just in time to see Eddy wink.

"Sure. Professional. Whatever you say, Jane-bug. If y'all are heading inside, I might sit with you, though, if you don't mind, since this is just a *professional* relationship." He grinned, as if he didn't believe it.

Cord's phone went off, and he pulled it from his pocket. "Excuse me, Eddy. I need to take this. Just one minute, Jane." He pushed the door open and stepped to the back of the truck.

"How long you guys been back together?" Eddy had one arm on the door of the truck, and he leaned inside. "You and Tarzan back there." He continued to grin.

"Two days ago, Eddy. I sprained my ankle, and Cord drove me to the hospital, that's all. But we'll catch up inside. I want to know everything that you've been up to since your rodeo team days."

"You remember that?" He laughed and slapped his leg. "Doesn't anyone remember that I was also on the Calculus Team? We went to state, but no one remembers that. Funny." He turned as Cord walked up to him.

"That was Veronica."

"Veronica?" Eddy looked puzzled.

"My daughter. She thinks the hacienda should be finished, all because I've been working on it for a couple of weeks. She doesn't know my skill level at carpentry. I didn't know my skill level." He laughed. "Nonexistent. However, the grandkids are begging to come out. They've never seen the ranch.

"I told her it would be at least another two, possibly three weeks before I would even want them anywhere near. Too dangerous with exposed wires and nails everywhere. We are going to have exposed wires and nails everywhere, right Jane?" He looked at her with a grin.

"If you'll help me out of this truck and into that shiny new DQ that I didn't know existed. Maybe I'll get to it, if I can ever get my coffee. You did ask them to wait?"

She didn't need his daughter around, not with the state she was in. It was that grin. It was melting her heart once again, and she didn't want it to. Not and leave her in the cold like before.

"Veronica understands, but since they're out of school for a few days, she was looking for something to do. She had her hopes up, but I suggested she rein in the team for another couple weeks."

"Coffee's sounding pretty good. Hey, guys, with seeing you again, I'm paying. Lunch is on me. Come on in. Cord, Jane?" Eddy waved them his direction and headed inside.

"Be right there." Cord leaned into the truck. "She really wants me to babysit. Veronica and Josh would probably enjoy the quiet without the boys. I told her as soon as the house is habitable, I'll have them down for a week. I think you'd like them, Jane. They're good boys, even if they are a little high spirited."

"I've got a couple just like that. Now, if you want to help someone out, that might be me, and to do that, I need you on this side of the truck. Come on, Tarzan. Help Jane out."

She laughed, using Eddy's monikers, but the memories those names brought back were bright, warm, and entirely too real. It was Eddy, she guessed, bridging the connection to all those years ago. It wasn't going to work, though. Cord wasn't going to use his daughter and his grandchildren to woo her back into his life. Old memories were fun, but it was the reality of life that counted. Six weeks, Cord. Six weeks, and she was gone, just as he'd been gone from her life all those years ago. She'd be gone, and she'd never look back. He'd see what it was like.

She wouldn't be let down by Juan Cordello Rivera III ever again.

— 13 —

JANE PULLED INTO THE drive winding up to Cord's home, pleased that at least the three days she'd been stranded at home hadn't been wasted. It felt good to be back on the job. With a six-week timetable to get the remodel completed, not even three days could be allowed to slip by without whip and mega-phone driving the progress forward.

Three days of barbeque and DQ breakfast sand-wiches hadn't helped, either, not her waistline, any-way. And she hadn't been able to convince Cord that a boiled egg and toast would feed her just fine.

Still, it was better than Bill. When she'd broken her arm at the skating rink, he'd hired a maid service, rather than lift a finger to help her out. The maid? Appreciated. She'd rather have had Bill's help, though.

With Cord? While the attention was nice, the feelings that ratcheted up anytime he came over left her jittery and unable to calm down afterward. Not exactly appropriate feelings for a recent widow.

Even Peggy's visits hadn't helped. She kept prodding her to be nicer to Cord. Goodness! If she were any nicer, she'd have to invite him to move in!

Billy had been her lifesaver. He'd called the second night while Cord was there, unaware of her injury, and he'd demanded to know all about the new job and the extent of her injury. His voice had set her straight. It had reminded her of Bill, and that had cleared the emotional overtones from the room.

Thank God for Billy.

"Jerry!" She rolled her window down and yelled to her foreman, Jerry Vanagas. "Good morning!" She pulled her Lexus next to where he stood with a set of plans unrolled on the hood of his truck and pushed the door open.

"Good morning, Mrs. Waggoner. We have made good progress, even without you here driving us forward." He spoke formally, with each word carefully enunciated, although the two knew each other well. It was his early background steeped in Mexican culture that was the cause, but his words were said with a smile.

"That's why you're my best." She pulled herself out of the car, using the door to balance. "I see the plans came through. When did you get them?"

"Two days ago. The walls, they were already torn out, and I had begun to worry. Then, this showed up, and there was no more problem. All will be beautiful." He smiled, his teeth white against his brown complexion. "And you, you are walking, but not well."

"Oh, I'm walking pretty well, Jerry. Just not fast. You don't worry about me. You worry about putting all those walls back right where those plans say." The plans weren't detailed, and they would be useless for anyone who wasn't Jerry. But they'd worked together on too many projects, and when she said bathroom, he knew where she would want plugs, drains, and lights, and she never had to worry.

Choosing the correct tiles and colors? There she had to worry, but that's why she got the big bucks, because she took big risks in pleasing her high-profile clients.

The house was a beehive of activity. The damaged roof tiles Cord had been working on were on the ground, and new, undamaged ones were in their place. A team was still working on one corner, applying a new layer of stucco. In a few days, it would be ready for paint, something rich and sandy to complement the dark wood trim.

"Ah, Jane!"

A voice called to her, and at first her heart raced, as she turned looking for Cord. She was disappointed. No, she told herself, *surprised* to see it was Lester Fortinbras, her trim man. The entire interior needed done, and several places outside had early rot. But that's why she had him on board, to get that ripped out and rebuilt.

"Les! Give me a minute. I'm a slow, old woman today. You heard about my ankle."

"I can see it." He nodded. It was wrapped nearly to her knee. "Several years back, my wife did the same thing. She was out of commission for a month. Surprising, you being out here today." He chuckled. "Tells me that Margie maybe could have been back to cooking long before she did."

"Don't start that, Les. You leave Margie alone. This still hurts, and a lot, too. How'd the porch columns come along? And the door? Did we have to replace the whole thing?"

"The columns," he started, slapping the closest one. They were mammoth-size twisted wood columns imported a century before from Mexico. "Three were pretty good, with only a little rot at the bottom. That one?" He pointed to the last of the four. "Eaten up with critters. Had to rip it out." He paused grinning.

"And?" It looked the same as the others. There was no way he could have gotten one shipped in this quickly, not and get it installed, too. It even had weathering that matched the ones that were original. "What did you do, Les? Steal one from a house in Westover?" She referred to the priciest, old money residential subdivision in the city of Fort Worth.

"You know the guesthouse." His eyes twinkled.

"I know the guesthouse. Just tell me, Les. Five

and a half weeks, and this must be finished. What about the guesthouse?"

"Those two half-relief columns? Remember those?" He grinned.

"You . . ." She stepped onto the porch and walked slowly that way, wishing she could go faster. If he did what she thought he did, it was brilliant. But what did that leave her on the guesthouse? "Don't tell me you patched this together from those."

"Okay, I won't, but where else was I to get one of these? They don't even make artisans that can carve these, at least not in Texas. Can you find the seam?" He was clearly very proud of his handiwork.

"You think that these might have once been . . ." She reached and traced the graining. "Here. This is the seam, right?" She turned to him and saw him nod, smiling broadly. "No. We couldn't be that lucky. You mean these were originally one column, and it was cut in half for the guesthouse? We couldn't be that lucky."

"Not lucky. You always say it, and you've about got me convinced. God watched over us—"

As Les said those words, she caught movement across the yard, and she glanced up to see Cord. He was carrying lumber, the boards balanced on his shoulder, clearly unaware she was there. His tee shirt was dirty and stained with sweat, but he was laughing at something the men with him had said. She wished she believed God had been watching over her forty years ago. Right now she wasn't so sure.

"—because there I was, out back moaning about how disappointed you'd be, and there these were. I knew, I don't know how, that these had to be a match, and being under the portico, they were pristine. We pulled them down, and mated together, the graining told the tale. Brother and sister reunited—"

Brother and sister reunited. It was the reunited part that caught Jane's attention, seeing Cord, and thinking about the times they'd had here on the ranch. She was heartsick, because he was there, and she was here, and that's all it was. That's all it could ever be. The past never came back, no matter how many times one called to it.

"Inside, Les." She turned from the column, needing an immediate diversion. "What's been done in there?"

"Oh, right. Lots, but only in some of the rooms. We're working on the dining room right now. That tin? We've only lost two panels, so far, and I think I've got someone lined up who can replicate them exactly. What do you think of that?"

She started to say he was wonderful, but another voice interrupted her.

"Well, what do you think? I suppose you *can* teach an old dog a new trick." Cord beamed, clearly proud of the massive efforts that had been made on the old hacienda.

That threw her off kilter. She thought he was still on the other side of the yard. Yet, here he was, stained and laughing and obviously excited about being back at the old place.

She didn't dare think it might have anything to do with talking to her.

She spoke more firmly than she might have otherwise, keeping a firm grip on the tremor she heard in her voice. "It's beginning to really take shape on the outside. Now, you've got to concentrate on the inside and getting the guesthouse rebuilt. You seem to be missing some trim."

He laughed. "You mean the columns. Yeah. I saw those, and I told Les to rip them off. I'd always thought they came from one piece. He didn't believe me, but I insisted, and I was right. Pretty amazing, huh?" He grinned.

"Les?" She turned. "You knew, and you didn't know how?"

He dropped his head and grinned. "I didn't say *how* I knew."

"Oh, did I say something I shouldn't? My apologies, Les." Cord didn't look repentant at all. "Oh, Jane, I think I'm mistaken. I remember how it happened, now. Why, there were Les and me, chewing the fat out back—only after a hard day's work, of course—and he said to me, I am in need of a replacement column, and I think these might do the trick. From there, it was the hand of God directing Les' every motion, from pulling those suckers down to gluing them back together again."

Les was laughing by then. "Not exactly, but I'll take it."

Jane felt herself caught up in Cord's charming rendition, laughing at his hokey phraseology, and enjoying the camaraderie between the two men, and before she caught herself, she thought, *I really should marry you, Cord Rivera. I would love to spend the rest of my life with you.*

She turned away, feeling sudden heat fill her face. The laughter was gone, and she felt tears threatening to overwhelm her. No. This was too much. She didn't want to marry Cord. He'd betrayed her, and another man had come along to rescue her from the detritus of her abandonment.

Then she turned back to Cord, his story still on, bantering with Les about the details involved. She pretended she was crying with laughter, but it was guilt. She felt she was betraying the man she was married to for nearly forty years. The questions of what if, would I, and should I hunkered on her shoulders, weighing her down. She pressed them back, but they only surged into her consciousness once more.

Did I really marry Bill only so that little Billy would have a real family? Would I have married him if he hadn't had that poor, wide-eyed little boy, so cute, so darling, and so much like the child she could no longer hold?

Had she been that empty? That little boy had loved her unconditionally, and in her loss, she had needed that. His father? At least he had given her free reign with his son, even if he hadn't been the father he could have been.

The husband, either, but he was dead now, and she wouldn't think of him that way. It was dishonest and mean, dirty, even, to think ill of the dead.

It was hard not to make the comparison, though, with Cord standing feet from her, roughed up and dirty, charming one of her workmen, and, she had to admit, charming her.

Oh! This was so much easier when she didn't have to spend time with him. Her grudges were so much easier to carry around when he wasn't nearby to work his way into her heart.

Then, unbidden, as if she needed to be reminded, the cover of *13 Weeks with Jesus* popped into her head. It showed a grand piano in front of a stained-glass window. There was an Oriental rug on the floor. It was beautiful. It was the words that went along with the image that yanked at her heart.

Forgive. Forget. Don't be angry. Love.

"I can't, Jesus," she whispered, so softly she was sure no one heard. "I can't do all that, not after forty years." She looked at Cord, laughing, and she wanted to. God help her, in that moment, she wanted to. Yet, she had lost too much, given up something very precious all those years ago, and how could she ever get that back? She couldn't forgive, could she? Not this.

The ache made her burn inside with indecision.

Forgive. Forget. Don't be angry. Love.

The words wouldn't go away, and Jane didn't know how she could do five and a half more weeks. She couldn't do it. Not at all.

— 14 —

"JANE? ARE YOU BUSY?" The words filtered through the dusty air.

Jane lifted the short board from the plans in front of her, letting the sheaf of papers snap into a tightly rolled tube. She glanced around, relieved at having a break in the day. The house was coming along, with floors torn up and patched, and new plaster on many of the interior walls.

The countertops had been the only sticking point. Cord had left everything else up to her judgment except that. She had argued with him that a lighter color would contrast better with the dark wood in the rest of the room, and she'd had to bring in multiple samples before he'd conceded her expertise on the topic.

She was about to decide she'd read something

more into his intentions than she should. Maybe she'd wanted something more. However, he'd been nothing if not proper and well-mannered, even preoccupied at times. He'd kept out of her hair, mostly, although the emails, texts, and phone calls sometimes ate up minutes a day—minutes she didn't have if she was to finish in only three weeks.

"In here, Cord." She turned, remembering the misstep she had made here all those weeks ago, and how it'd left her ankle sore for two weeks. That weak spot in the threshold was the first thing she'd had repaired.

"In here, you little varmints." Cord leaned into the room, smiling. "I brought you a little company." He disappeared again, but the sound of running feet and laughter echoed in the empty rooms.

"Company?" Jane took a deep breath. *Little* company she didn't need. Billy provided her plenty of that when she kept the babies, although she knew they weren't babies any longer. They just acted like it.

A woman Jane didn't recognize appeared in the doorway, and she smiled, reaching out to catch a small boy by the hand just as he darted by. She had strawberry blonde hair, and a spattering of freckles tickled her nose. The boy was equally light.

Then Cord stepped into view, holding another boy about the same as the first under his arm. The boy squirmed, but he was laughing at the same time.

"I told you they were restless little critters." Cord grinned. "This one's J-4, and that's one's Gabe."

"I'm Gabe," the one under his arm squealed.

"Oh, you are?" Cord laughed. "I know what Gabe sounds like. Let's see if you sound like him." He dug his fingers into the boy's side, grinning at Jane when he squirmed and howled in mock pain.

"Ow, ow! I'm Gabe! Promise, Granddaddy!"

"I guess you are." Cord dropped him unceremoniously. "Promise, Jane, I can't tell the difference unless they howl. Gabe howls louder."

"Daddy, stop it. Introduce me to your designer." The woman turned to Jane. "This is amazing, you know. I remember the place, but it's been twenty-five or thirty years. I don't remember it like this."

"I've changed it a bit." Jane looked from father to daughter, finding no resemblance at all. "You're, um, Veronica, right?"

"Daddy! What do you two talk about? I at least thought you would have shown her my picture." Just then, J-4 tore lose, chasing after his brother. "I'm sorry. I'll be right back. They'll break something if I don't keep them corralled." She disappeared the direction of the boys.

"Told you." Cord grinned.

"That's Veronica?"

"None other. And my grandbabies. Chip off somebody's block, tell you that. I never was so wild as a kid. At least I tell people that." He'd walked up beside her, and he unrolled the papers she'd had out. "Kitchen? Is that granite here, yet? I want to see a big slice."

"All in. Do you want to wait on your daughter?"

"Veronica?" He yelled her name. "We're headed into the kitchen."

"That's how you do it?" Jane laughed. "You just yell?"

He winked. "Works. With those kids, no telling where I'd find her. Come on. Let's get out of here while we have the chance. The little tornados might be back any time."

Despite herself, Jane felt lighter, as if she wanted to run into the kitchen with Cord and hide. She had to put the brakes on that impulse, but it somehow *felt* right, even if she knew it was no good.

She and Cord were no good. That'd proven itself forty years ago. However, for the moment, caught up in his escape, she followed him to the kitchen.

"Hey, look at this." The granite, honey gold, stretched for what seemed acres. "I like this." He ran a hand over the surface, lifting it to see his palm coated with dust.

"Everything's dusty in here and will be until we're finished. It's coming along, though."

"So, what's with the kitchen plans? This looks about done to me." He reached up and grabbed a dangling light fixture, one designed to be recessed into the ceiling. " 'Cept this, of course." He smiled.

"I'm reworking the cabinets under the sink. I decided to upgrade to a tankless water heater, and the model I've chosen doesn't want to fit. It will, though." She leaned against the cabinet, crossing her arms across her chest and her legs at the ankles. "I'm good at this. I might even get it finished by the reunion."

"You might, huh?"

Several men lumbered in through the door, carrying a large wood beam. They were speaking rapidly in Spanish and kicking things out of the way.

"Pedro! Sammy! The boss is here!" Jane waved at them.

"Ah, Mr. Rivera." The men set their beam down on two sawhorses, and wiping their hands on their pants, they stepped forward to shake. "Our hands, they are not freshly washed, but please shake with us. We are pleased to meet the owner of such a fine establishment. This will make you and Mrs. Waggoner a good home."

Only one of the men spoke, but the second murmured, "Si, senor. Verdaderamente excelente!"

Jane felt her face go hot. "No, no, Sammy. Not ours. It belongs only to Mr. Rivera."

"Ah! Only yours?" He pointed to Cord. "Such a big home for one man. So very sad. Perhaps someday?" He motioned between them with his hand. "Algún día?" He had a hopeful look on his face.

Jane knew enough Spanish to understand his question. "No, not algún día." She couldn't even look at Cord. She did hear Sammy turn to Pedro and speak in rapid-fire Spanish. She only caught a few of the words, but it was clear he was explaining that the happy marriage was not to take place after all.

"Happy marriage?"

She looked at Cord to see him smiling broadly. Oh, God, what was this going to turn into? She'd forgotten he was fluent in Spanish. He must think she'd been telling the workers they were getting married. All she'd said was that Mr. Rivera *might* get married someday, and the house had to have at least a bit of a woman's touch.

This was going to go downhill quickly!

"I never said that, Cord." She turned to glare at Pedro and Sammie, but Pedro had such a sad look on his face that she almost wanted to give him a hug and tell him it would be all right.

Instead, Pedro turned around and walked back out the door, muttering, "Muy triste."

"Pedro is sad. Very sad." Sammy held his hands up, palms out, as if in apology. "We will go be busy. You have much to say to one another, I am sure." But he winked as he backed away.

"Jane?" Cord turned to her. "What was that about?"

"I have no idea. None. Trust me." She laughed, and couldn't believe she did. A nervous reaction, she figured. "I'm glad your daughter wasn't in here to hear that. My goodness, what would she think?"

"About what?" Veronica came struggling through the door, pulling one boy by the arm, and with the second hiked up on her waist. "Here, Dad, this one's yours." She leaned the one on her hip to Cord, letting go as soon as her dad had his hands on him. "Now, you, buster, you've kicked me the last time. Do you want me to lock you in the car?"

"She wouldn't really," Cord mouthed at Jane. "It works, though." Indeed the boy quieted, although he had a bit of a sulk on his face.

"So, which one are you?" Jane stepped to the boy, glad to have something to do besides discuss her workmen's social gaffes. "Is it Gabe, or are you," and she looked up at Veronica, "C-4?"

"I'm J-4," the boy said, then he buried his head against his mother."

"So, I've got Gabe again." Cord looked at the boy in his arms. "I might need to test the siren and make sure."

"No, Granddaddy," the boy yelled, throwing his arms around Cord's neck. "Don't, please!"

"Just a little?" He touched the boy's side with one finger.

"It's really me," Gabe squealed, thrashing his legs.

"Okay. Now that I'm sure. Although, if I make the other one squeal, then I'll know for certain."

The boy at Veronica's side grabbed his mother, hiding behind her. "No, Granddaddy. Please, Mommy?"

"Granddaddy, don't tease like that." Veronica patted J-4's head. "They're just kids."

"Nitro-glycerin on two legs, but you're right, as usual. I'll back off."

"Thank you, Daddy." She reached up and gave

him a kiss on the cheek, then she turned to Jane. "Daddy's told me all about you, despite the fact he hasn't said a thing about me. Some daddy, huh?" But she laughed. "I feel I know you already."

"He did talk about you some, but I expected . . . well, maybe a bit more of your father's looks. You must take after your mother." It had been forty years, but Jane couldn't seem to recall Shelly with strawberry blonde hair. Oh, well. Shelly hadn't been one of her close friends, and who knew where the genes were hiding for that fair skin. Not with Cord, unless through his mother. She was Irish, after all.

"Jane, are you there?"

She looked at Cord. "I'm sorry. I was thinking of your mother. Didn't she have red hair?"

"Don't worry about it." He winked. "You'll never figure it out. Now, though, I want to show Veronica the house. Want to tag along?"

"Three weeks is all he's given me to finish." Jane reached to touch Veronica gently on the arm. She laughed. "If I get off track even one minute, it'll never get done, and your father will never forgive me."

"Oh, he'll forgive you, all right. You're the best thing that's happened to Daddy since I can remember. You're all he talks about. Thank you."

That took Jane aback. It sounded like Veronica expected her and Cord to be more than just business partners. Surely not! However, it was what Veronica said as she and her father stepped into the other room that really got Jane's goat.

"Do you think she suspects anything?"

"Shush! I haven't said a word."

"What word, Granddaddy?"

That was J-4, and Cord reached down and wrapped him in his free arm, tossing him over his shoulder.

"My word, you little wildebeest. And I say you're all shook up!" As they disappeared, Cord rocked him back and forth, leaving the boy howling with laughter.

Suspects what? Jane frowned. Oh, well, she had a house to finish, and she hadn't been teasing with Veronica. She didn't have an hour to spare. She turned to her rolled paper and frowned at the space under the sink that didn't quite want to accommodate the tankless water heater that Jane was determined to fit there.

And it would go, if she had to take a Sawzall to it herself.

— 15 —

JANE PULLED UP TO the jobsite, her engine running, and the lights cutting across the new concrete drive. There were bushes and shrubs carefully organized off to the side. She knew it was carefully, because she'd been the one to stand there and point out where the nursery was to place them, the first to go in on the outside; the last to be installed at the back.

All those bushes presented a problem, too. They blocked the drive, or at least the part that took her directly to the guesthouse. She would be forced to divert through the main residence.

She clicked her cheek when she saw a light go on in the main house. She watched the window—there were no curtains or blinds in yet—to see who it was. Cord, possibly, or his daughter or grandchildren, at an outside chance. She shook her head. He wanted this completed in a week, then had decided to move in and slow everything down. If she'd known that, she'd have focused more energy on the guesthouse, rather than leaving it for last. He wouldn't have been in anyone's way there.

Still, the house was Cord's, and he did pull the strings, financial as well as otherwise. The ones on her heart? She didn't dare answer that question. Not after five weeks of working at his side. She might make another mistake, and she couldn't afford another four decades of living with the consequences.

Now he wanted her in the guesthouse. *You'll get so much more work done.* Right. Yet, there were her things in the back seat, her swatches and paint samples, as well as a small suitcase and an overnight bag.

Was she a fool, or was she a fool? Toss the coin up, and either way it fell, the odds were the same.

Well, the guesthouse didn't have to be complete for her. The windows were in, and mid-May, the air systems didn't matter much. That was on tap for this week, and she had a fan until then.

She didn't need a kitchen. Cord had offered his, sort of a test run to see if everything was in working order. It had made sense, in an off-kilter sort of way. She wasn't sure her back would appreciate the air bed in the trunk, but she'd last, she thought. A week? Who couldn't manage that?

The hard thing? She was growing very attached to this old house. She usually enjoyed her projects, even wondered if they were places she would enjoy living, but this? She had wanted this life all those years ago, and now here she was remaking it into whatever she wanted it to be. Even those feminine touches she'd wanted, the small things like the shell soap holders in the half bath. Her own special touches, ones that would hopefully be appreciated by the future woman of the house.

Whoever married Cord.

"Not me." She cleared her throat. "Cord Rivera, you keep to your side of the breezeway, and I'll keep to mine. Kitchen's neutral ground, and don't you forget it." She wouldn't have done this for any other person, and she was quite aware, she shouldn't be doing it for this one.

She killed the car, opening the door and pulling her things from the back. By the time she got to the house, she knew her ankle wasn't as well as she tried to convince herself. By the time she fumbled the front door open, Cord, stocking feet and pajamas, was there to greet her.

"Hey, moving in, I see." He grinned. "I've got coffee and toast in the kitchen."

"Not moving in," She growled. It sounded so salacious that way. She didn't need salacious. "The drive to the guesthouse is blocked with plantings. I've got to cut through. Here, take these." She handed him the cases. "I've got my bed in the car." She turned to head back outside.

"You can sleep in the guesthouse. That's why I

offered it to you." Amusement filled the words.

"I intend to." She didn't turn, the connotations in his words working her emotions. "What else did you have in mind?"

"Your bed . . . in the car. I didn't mean, um, it was just a joke." He coughed, as if with embarrassment, or perhaps an off-hand apology. She couldn't tell which.

"Thank you at six-thirty in the morning. I like my jokes at ten. I'll be right back." She stepped outside, pulling the door tightly to. Her words had been sharp, but it was to cover her heart. It was swelled inside her, choking her mind, and keeping her from thinking straight.

And why had that man still been in his pajamas? He knew she was coming over about sunup, and the sun would be up in another half hour. What was she supposed to do, sit at home and wait for him to call? Oh, wait, she'd done that at eighteen. Only he never had, and then he had married someone else, never coming to see her or contact her in all those years.

Like he'd been too happy to care.

She was digging in her trunk, blinking the tears away, when she heard a voice at her side.

"Anything I can carry?"

Gracious, Cord, here I am sniveling into my trunk, and I don't even have a tissue. How could this morning go even further down the tube?

"This." She handed him the box containing the airbed without turning. "I have to set that up."

"This?" He held it under the trunk light. "You

— 135 —

can't sleep on this. I'll—"

"You'll what?" She turned to him, drawing her sleeve across her face as if wiping away sweat. It was for her tears, though. "You invited me. You going to swing a hammock between two trees? That'd be a sight, me sleeping in the out-of-doors in my p.j.s. I do wear p.j.s, you know."

Cord laughed. "Whoa, missy. I don't even have a hammock, that is unless you ordered one in and it got delivered without me knowing it. I was thinking, I could take the guesthouse, and you could have my room. Just for the week. It'd all be honest and above-board." He leaned against the car, holding the bed in his arms like a baby.

"Don't you think you're doing that to me, Cord Rivera." She chuckled, but it wasn't in amusement. "I'm here to help you get done on time, but nothing else. Is that plain?"

"Jane." He set the box back in the trunk. "What have I done that you don't trust me? What? Have I kissed you or in any way compromised you, or even suggested it?"

"Now or then?" He had. Not this spring, but on a long-ago spring, very much so.

"Ouch. Again."

"Why again?" She felt her heart strings, and he was yanking them. Maybe this wasn't such a good idea.

"Five weeks ago, you said something similar. It hit home then, and it hits home now." He stopped, looking away.

"Okay, Cord Rivera. I have no idea what I said five weeks ago. You remember. What made it so important that something I said stuck with you?" She crossed her arms and leaned against the car, really wanting to hear this.

"Jane, you think you're not important to me, but you are. Forty years ago, our world fell apart, and I know who was to blame. I've beat myself up for decades. I can't do that anymore, and when you remind me, it's like a knife, hot, serrated, and buttered, slipping inside and taking my heart out all over again."

Jane couldn't talk, and she was glad the sun wasn't quite up. How could that man peel back forty years so easily, as if it were a blanket, and all those years were lying underneath, just waiting to come to life again? Her heart in her throat, she reached for the bed.

"Can't leave this. I'll need it tonight." She felt the huskiness in her voice, and she didn't want to be betrayed. She turned away and marched toward the house. "Shut the trunk. I'm finished in there."

He'd almost given her an apology. That's all she'd wanted, just for Cord to acknowledge the pain he'd put her through. She could almost love him for that.

Almost, but not yet. That water under the bridge hadn't quite made it back to her heart, yet.

"BILLY! IT'S NOT EVEN seven. How did you

know I'd be up?" Jane looked out the window to see Cord heading toward the house.

"Mom! When are you not up before seven? Besides, Aunt Peggy said you were headed to work early, and you'd be out at the old Rivera place all week. The kids want to come out and see you. Jasmine, too. She knows she'll never get to see the infamous house, if she doesn't get an invite before you wrap things up. When it comes out in D magazine, she wants to tell people she was there in person with the designer." He chuckled.

"I'll ask, honey. Maybe the day of the reunion. How about then?" She turned at the sound of the door.

"What are you asking me?" Cord winked at her.

She covered the mouthpiece. "Who said I was asking you anything?"

"You said you'd ask honey. That's me, right?" Cord grinned.

"Oh, shush!" She smiled, waving him away. "This is Billy, my son."

"Hey, Billy!" Cord called loudly enough to carry over the phone.

"Mom? Who's that?"

"The homeowner, son. He's out here with me."

"At seven in the morning?" He chuckled.

"Not all of us can get up at nine. Sorry. And we must start early if we're finishing by the weekend. I'll get with you later today. Bye, sweetie." She palmed the phone off as she slid it into her bag.

"So, what are you asking?" Cord still stood in the same place.

"My daughter-in-law, Jasmine, wants to see the house before I turn it over to you. Do you mind?"

"It's not finished, yet. Does she have a brilliant imagination?" He fought a smile. "Then, if she's pretty as you, she can stay the entire week, and she'll get to see it in its final form. You might even persuade her to help. Does she paint?"

"You fool." Jane laughed. "She's twenty-three years younger than me. Of course, she's prettier. Besides, she can't hold a brush, not unless it has makeup on it. At that? She's quite skilled." She pushed the bed's box aside with her foot. "Billy was saying this weekend. Maybe before the reunion. They'll have the kids, I'm afraid, but they can come early and be gone before it starts."

"They can come anytime. My grandkids will be here. Throw yours in, and it'll be like a bunch of little Cheetahs in here." Cord laughed, and his eyes lit up.

That made Jane giggle. "Little Cheetahs? Well, Tarzan, I don't think we're done here, yet. There are still a lot of loose ends to finish up. You'll have to wait a little while longer before you can swing through the trees with Cheetah."

"Thank you, Jane." Cord had a wide smile on his face.

"For what?" She was still trying to get her smile wiped away.

"For laughing with me. It was almost like old

times. My house" —he motioned all around him— "is beautiful, but without you in it . . ." He stopped and looked at the ceiling, his eyes red.

"What, Cord?" She watched him expectantly.

He laughed, wiping his hands across his face, the tracks of his hands glistening. "I'd rather swing through the trees with Jane any day than with a silly monkey." He laughed again. "Well, that shows what a fool I am."

"Typical male, always ready to hang out with the girls when there's work to be done." Stupid comeback, but his words certainly caught her off guard. Unable to deal with any more, she grabbed her box and walked away, calling back to him over her shoulder, "I'll be in the laundry room and office if you need me."

Swing through the trees with Jane! However, his comment pleased her more than she intended to let on.

— 16 —

"ARRGH!" JANE RAN HER fingers through her hair. "May! In Texas!"

It was the humidity. It had rained three times in two days, and her hair had become a wild mess, uncontrollable and in her way. And she didn't have time to roll it and set it. Not and get this job finished.

Even that wouldn't bother her if everything wasn't going wrong. The air installer had brought the wrong compressor for the guesthouse, none of her hand-drawn sketches were matching deliveries, and oh! In the distance, more rain threatened, with black clouds hovering against the horizon. Of all days! The landscapers were due that afternoon to plant hundreds of shrubs. They had to go in by Saturday. It was the day of the reunion.

She looked up at the sun, then at the shimmering pool. At least that was working, even though she couldn't take time for a dip. It was tempting, though. Very tempting. If she had a suit . . .

"Jane! Come take a break."

She looked at the main house to see Cord hanging out of the new French doors she'd had installed. *Sure, Cord. And it doesn't matter if the house is done or not.* Still, she waved and smiled. "Working! Sorry!"

"Hold on!" He disappeared. Through the glass, she could see him doing something in the kitchen. In moments, he stepped through the door holding two glasses.

"What's that?" *Duh! Obvious.*

"Your break. You won't come to it. It comes to you." He smiled that disarming, charming smile that got her in the stomach every time.

"It *is* hot. I'll give you that. Thanks." She reached for one of the glasses.

"No. Over here." He motioned with his head to the new chaise lounges that had come in that morning. "We have to try these out before it's too late to send them back. Sit with me." He placed the glasses on a small table centered between the chairs and adjusted the cushion on Jane's. He motioned and waited for her to sit before he fell back on his.

"This is good." She took a deep draw from one of the glasses. "The tree overhead is better." She laughed, and when she looked Cord's direction, he was smiling. "However, if I'm sitting here, I'm working."

"Jane. It's five minutes." He leaned his head back and closed his eyes. "Like this. You can do it."

"And not be finished on Saturday. We've got rain coming, or haven't you noticed?"

"I noticed, and I don't care. I've got what I want."

She looked at him sharply. There was a lot not done. He couldn't be so unobservant as that. "Tell me, then, if what I've accomplished pleases you so much, what do you like best about it?"

"You being here." His eyes were still closed, but he smiled when he said it.

"I should have expected that." It also felt good to hear him say it, but it wasn't what she wanted to hear. "About the remodel." She chuckled. Men, so single minded.

"These chairs." He shifted position. "Yes, definitely. These chairs."

"Not the granite? Or, how about that tankless water heater. I spent hours figuring that out."

"Soap holders."

"Soap holders? You're spending hundreds of thousands here, and the soap holders are what you like best?" She laughed out loud. "Describe them for me." She had to hear this.

"That big." He held up his hands, making a circle, his eyes still closed. "Scalloped, like a shell, and very feminine."

"So you *were* paying attention."

"Oh, trust me, Jane. I've been paying attention."

He chuckled.

"Oh, I bet you have. Back to the house. What's not finished?" Had he even noticed? Well, her air in the guesthouse, but he had working air in the main house. He wouldn't know about hers.

"Us." He lifted his glass and took a sip of tea.

"Cord, get on track. I'm talking business. What have I not yet finished with the house?" He was actually being pretty funny. She let herself lean back into the chase's cushion. This was nice, the pool, the tree, the shade, and talking to someone she enjoyed being around. She did like Cord. It was her trust that had been frayed beyond repair. Well, beyond simple and easy repair. Anything could be repaired, if people worked at it enough.

"Landscaping. Even a blind skunk could see that."

"Blind skunk?"

"I was, you know." His eyes were still closed.

"A blind skunk?"

"Me. All those years ago. I was a blind skunk. Stinking stupid. Except I got Veronica. I'd do it all differently, except for Veronica."

"And J-4 and Gabe?" She felt her heart pounding. This wasn't business, not by a country mile.

"The tornadoes?" He grinned. "They're up for debate."

"What do you mean you would do it differently?" She took a deep breath to calm herself. She cringed as she heard him start to answer.

"C'mon, Jane. You know what I mean." He

— 144 —

looked at her. "You and me. Can you tell me you wouldn't do our lives differently if you had the choice?"

She bit her bottom lip, afraid to speak. No, not afraid. Unable to speak. Would she, if it meant no Billy? She loved him, her only child, the one she'd treasured to replace the one she'd lost. Losing Cord had been the devastation of her life, but Billy had been her salvation.

"Jane? This is my last chance. I don't want you to leave this week without us at least talking. I mean really talking. The stuff that's important to us, that we should have said four decades ago, and we were, no, I was too immature to know I needed to say." He dropped his feet over the side of the chase, sitting up and facing her.

"I—" She looked at her tea. "I—" She couldn't get the words out.

"I know this is bold of me. I'm the one who abandoned you. I know that, and God knows how much I've kicked myself around for it. I can't change what I did, although God knows I wish I could. But one day. One real, honest day. Can you give me that?"

Can I? Can I give Cord one honest day? Does he really know what he's asking for? She swallowed, setting the glass aside. This chair, the shade, the pool, even, didn't look so inviting, anymore.

"Too much, huh?" Cord started to run his hand through his hair, and he stopped with his fingers buried. "Me. Bull in china shop. God, I'm stupid!" He slammed his hand down on the chaise, the noise softened by the cushion. "I have you here, even if it's just for six weeks, and I have to spoil it by bringing up the past. I'm sorry, Jane. After forty years, I still haven't learned anything."

"Grubstake. Six o'clock." She stood abruptly, her self-control almost slipping. "You drive, you pay, and you can have one evening. Not a whole day, but one evening. Then we'll see." She walked away, her eyes burning, and afraid to stand near him any longer.

She knew what he wanted. She wanted it, too, or she had years ago. She wanted to trust him, but there was something missing from the equation, something she had given up, and something she could never get back again. There would always be an empty space between Cord and her, and he would never know why.

If only she could back up forty years. Cord wasn't the only one that had made a mistake. She'd made one even bigger, and she couldn't tell anyone.

Not even Cord.

THE SHOWER HAD HELPED, standing under the cold water that wasn't really all that cold. No one could have told the difference between the tears and the water from the nozzle, and that was the way Jane wanted it. It also meant she could let the tears go, pretending they hadn't been cried at all.

Standing in front of the mirror, she patted her face dry, surprised at the person who stood on the other side. She didn't realize she'd been working so hard, but the person staring back at her was much trimmer than she had been since high school.

"Nerves!" She laughed. "Not the best diet in the world." She pulled her hair into a knot at the back of her neck, tying it up before opening her bag to scatter her makeup over the counter, glad she'd given in to Cord's offer to use the hacienda's guest bath. The refrigerated air was refreshing. Thinking of what Cord wanted to discuss wasn't.

Better wow him, she thought, lifting the dress she'd brought in. It was a soft blue with darker lines of peach infused with deeper hues of blue. She selected the matching make-up, intending to trowel it on a little heavier than usual. Night required that, didn't it, and it would be night before they returned.

"Ooh, Jane, quit being bitter. You had a life, and all that was two lifetimes ago, seen from the vantage point of a college kid. Get over it, and just enjoy the fact that Cord's paying, and you're getting a free meal."

The woman in the mirror didn't answer back. She stood mute, as if in reproof.

"I wouldn't talk to me, either. Sorry." She felt ashamed. She remembered what God had directed her to in her devotions. *Forgive. Forget. Don't be angry. Love.* She wanted to do the first. She could never do the second. The third always came back to haunt her, and the fourth? That was the one she had the most trouble with. She was already there, and she was determined not to give in to it.

Then, the woman in the mirror put on a bright face, applied the makeup a little heavier than she should, and sidled into a dress that would have been a size too small six weeks ago. Tonight it fit perfectly. She would be bright, cheerful, listen to whatever Cord had to say, and she would forgive, not be angry, and try to love the entire evening.

It was the forgetting that she refused to discuss. How could she forget what she had given away?

The dress did look good, though, and in her heavy-duty makeup, perhaps even Jasmine would get a run for her money. She slipped on her shoes and flung the door wide, determined to make the most of a very difficult evening.

"Jane!" Cord's word was a murmur, as if he couldn't believe the truth standing before him.

"What?" She checked to see if she had toilet tissue stuck to the sole of her shoe.

"You don't know, do you?" His smile grew wider. "You make Tarzan want to grab the biggest vine in the jungle and take Jane with him." He said it with a little laugh, releasing some of the tension.

"Oh, you're not getting off that easy, mister. You said you were buying my dinner," she shot back at him, forcing a smile. She felt some of the tension go out of her body. This was just Cord, and they were only having dinner.

Yes, that was it. They were only having dinner, and she would be the best date he'd ever had. That's what she would do, if it took every ounce of effort she possessed.

— 17 —

HUNGER. THAT'S ALL it'd been. Hunger.

Jane told herself that. She'd ordered grilled chicken chef salad, extra croutons, and unsweetened tea, and now Cord was plying her with cherry pie. She hadn't succumbed yet, but that hadn't stopped him from teasing her with mouthful after mouthful.

Now she was enjoying his company, rather than feeling sorry for herself. Hunger could do that, couldn't it?

"Jane, just a bite." Cord held a cherry on the end of a fork, his hand under it to catch any drips. "I haven't forgotten how you loved my mother's cherry pie." He pushed it at her encouragingly.

"No, don't." Jane held her hand in front of her face, laughing. "And don't you drip that on me, either. This is the first time I've worn this dress, and nothing on it is cherry red."

"But it would look good in cherry red. Cherry pie red." He turned the fork around and pulled the cherry off with his teeth. "Anyway, too late now, unless you want it the fun way." He showed her the cherry held between his teeth.

She turned her head, looking at the other diners to see if they were watching. She hissed between bouts of giggling, "Are you still in high school? Stop that and act like a grown-up. We're in public."

"So, if I order pie to go, I can do this back at the hacienda? As long as it's in private?" His eyes twinkled, and he fought a smile.

"Not with me in the same room."

"Then one bite, and I'll stop." He speared another cherry, this time with some crust attached. "Just one." He held it out to her.

"No. You men might be able to handle desserts, but us women? All it does is go to fat. I don't intend to be fat."

"That I can tell. Anyway, it's your loss." He ate the second bite. "It's really good."

About that time the check appeared, and the waitress said, "Pay at the front counter. Thank y'all, and y'all have a really good night. Just be careful of the rain. I think it's about to come a gusher." She nodded towards the windows.

"Cord, we'd better be going." Jane turned to the waitress. "Thank you for the warning. I might save

— 151 —

my hair after all."

"Glad to help, ma'am. You're pretty, and pretty women deserve to be made special by their husbands. Lucky you." She winked at Jane and tilted her head Cord's way.

"But, we're—" Jane wanted no misunderstanding.

Cord grabbed her hand and interrupted. "Thank you, Miss. That's worth an extra tip for sure." He winked at Jane. "I'll take good care of her, because she's special."

Jane chuckled, letting the girl's misunderstanding slide. She felt good tonight. Much better than earlier in the afternoon, and that was a relief. Cord was already standing, and she grabbed her clutch, pausing at the window and looking out as he paid. It looked like water drops on the sidewalk, but coming down? That she couldn't tell.

It was obvious when they stepped outside. A gust of wind tore past them, then large drops scattered across the pavement. She laughed, and Cord grabbed her arm and started to run. The Escalade beeped and flashed its lights just as they got to the door, and Jane scrambled in, just as the really big drops started. Cord ran to the other side, jumping in barely in time to miss the torrent that began to pound the vehicle.

"At least it's not hot any longer." Jane reached to Cord's shirt sleeve to touch the water spatters. "Not dry, either. Sorry."

"Oh, it's nothing. I'll dry, and this'll be good for the soil. Loosen it up for planting, although most people planning new gardens should have already done so." He pressed the starter on the dash, and the truck came to life, the engine almost silent against the sound of the rain.

"I'm glad you're driving." She pressed one hand to the window at her side. "I never did like getting out in rough weather." She looked at Cord. "How 'bout you?"

"Ever drive a Caddy?" He rapped the dash with his knuckles. "Magnetic Ride Control and—" he paused expectantly "—Stabilitrak traction control. Every driver's dream." He grinned. "Makes rough weather driving worries a thing of the past."

She smiled. "Then radio up, please. And home."

"Yes, ma'am." He touched several buttons on his steering wheel, and the sounds of a sixties' tune gently pulsed through the cabin.

"Nice." Jane worked her way into a comfortable position in the big, overstuffed, leather seat. "I remember this song."

"From?" Cord was pulling out onto the highway, with the wipers going full on.

"Us, remember?" She'd still been a junior, and she and Cord had been at the old DQ in line to order. The song had come on, and she'd sung it for the first time. How had she ever forgotten that?

"In my old truck?"

"At the DQ." She laughed. "You don't remember, do you?"

Instead of answering, he hummed along for a minute, then he reached for her hand. "I remember you. That's better."

"I bet." She pulled her hand away. "Focus on your driving."

"If I must." His voice was husky, though.

"You must." What was she doing? She should be on the far side of the truck, slapping his hand away. She couldn't, though. With the rain, and the song, it felt too right, and she didn't want it to end just yet.

It was ten minutes before they pulled off the road onto the new concrete drive leading up to the hacienda. Cord swung the big truck into the garage, and everything became quiet.

"We're here."

"And dry." Jane laughed.

"Barely. Come in for a minute?"

Jane looked outside at the rain pouring down. "Might be tough getting to the guesthouse in this."

"Even under the breezeway?" His words were soft, almost as if he needed to remind her of something.

"It's early, yet, and that rain is sideways. I'd get soaked, even under a roof. Sorry. You've got to put up with me for a while." It even seemed okay, her last chance to be in the big house as a guest. After all, come the weekend, and she'd be out of Cord's hair forever, and he'd be out of hers, even if it didn't seem quite so appealing as it had that afternoon.

"Let me put on a dry shirt, and we'll have a toast to a great evening. How does that sound, my novia?"

"I'm game." She shot him a "thumbs-up" sign of approval. It wasn't until she was climbing out of the truck that she paused, wondering if she'd been mistaken. Had he actually said *novia* at the end of his question? That was what he used to call her in high school, sweetheart in Spanish.

If so, it was very bittersweet.

Lightning crashed, and they dashed into the house, letting the garage door close off the storm outside. A second crash, and the lights flickered, but they stayed on.

"Candles, Cord?"

He raised his hands in a defensive gesture. "I just write the checks. All this is yours. You tell me."

"That's a man for you." Jane began going through the kitchen cabinets. "Surely you've moved *something* in here. If not, it's going to get awfully dark if we lose electricity."

"Okay. Wait a minute." He stepped down a hallway and returned with a plastic crate. "Veronica brought this in yesterday. Just maybe . . ." He began to dig.

Another crash of thunder, and the lights flickered again, then died.

"Cord? Candles?" Jane could see him in snatches, when lightning gave her brief glances.

"Hang on." He continued to dig.

"It's dark. I don't like the dark much."

"A-ha!" A flame erupted, and then there was another and another.

"They're awfully small." But they were light, and for that, Jane was glad.

"Birthday candles. My grandsons' is coming up, and these are the party decorations."

"You're burning their birthday candles?"

He laughed. "I can get more. Besides, we need them now." He had already moved to the kitchen and was pulling long-stemmed glasses from a cabinet.

"Can I transfer them to the living room?"

"Sure. I'm just looking for the bottle opener."

"I need a plate."

He pulled out one and handed it to her as he dug through a drawer. As soon as she took it, he yelled, "Jackpot!" He turned with an opener in his hand. "What's the plate for?"

"I'm not holding those candles, and if you've never noticed, those little things burn out in about ten minutes. If the power stays off, we'll be using a lot of them."

"Gotcha. There's an extra box in the crate. Get 'em if you think we need 'em. I'll get the toast ready." He pulled a bottle from the fridge.

"Ow, ow!" One of the candles sputtered out. "We lost one." She was laughing, though.

"Here." He reached in the crate and tossed her the fresh box. "Gotta keep the supply up."

"Like camping out." She grinned.

"A first. We never did that, did we?"

"What do you mean?"

"As kids. We were always so busy. Never enough

time to do all the things we wanted to do."

"What about the junior weenie roast? That big bonfire, and everyone stayed over half the night." She giggled. "My dad was so mad he could spit. It was only two, and he thought we'd been out all night."

"Doesn't count. This'll be our first, camping out with candles for our campfire." He grinned, setting two glasses on the coffee table.

"Makes a pretty wimpy campfire." She laughed. It was pretty, though, the house lighted with little candles.

"I appreciate this, Jane." Cord picked up his glass, and he swirled the liquid inside. "You, me, here."

"Thank you." She picked up hers. "Toast?"

"Not yet. What I meant was that I appreciate you spending the evening with me. Just us. I've wanted to do this for a long time."

"Cord, be careful. I've had fun, and I don't want it spoiled." With his tone, she hadn't much hope, though.

"We have to talk, Jane." When she made to interrupt him, he held up his hand. "No, listen. I want to tell you the truth. It's time you heard it from me." He took a deep breath and downed the liquid in his glass. "Oh, right, that was for our toast. Sorry." He grinned sheepishly.

"Cord—" she began, not wanting to hear what he had to say. *Four days and we're done. Don't spoil it now, Cord. Don't you do it.*

"I never cheated on you back then."

His face looked like he'd said something he'd wanted to say for a very long time. Relief? Jane couldn't tell, but she did know what she thought about his words. She felt her reaction boil up inside of her, and her emotions exploded with violence.

"What do you mean you never cheated on me? Of course you cheated on me—with Shelly. She was easy, and you just couldn't keep your hands off her. You had to have a piece of her like every other guy in town." Jane spit the words at him like they were venom. This whole perfect evening, and he had to ruin it with this. She had *known* he would do this. She had *known* it! How could she have been such a fool!

And, how could he look at her with that shocked expression after he lied like that? She turned from him, her glass still in her hand, the liquid inside quivering with her rage. If he only had the decency to tell her the truth, she could live with that. Not this. He thought he could lie, and it would all go away. No. He had broken her heart once, and that was enough.

She felt relief flood over her. She'd almost let it happen again. Now she knew, and everything was in the open where it should be. Then the anger boiled up again.

"Oh!" she cried, turning to him, pointing with her glass, shaking it with fury. "How could you, you, you, you *man,* you!"

Then she burst into tears, unable to contain the pain of Cord's betrayal any longer.

— 18 —

"JANE, PLEASE. HEAR ME out before you get your defenses up." Cord had hoped, really hoped that their evening together, their very pleasant evening together, would ameliorate the moment of his declaration.

What he got was more what he'd expected. Before he could put together more than his lame—even he had to admit that—rebuttal, Jane fired off a volley of anger to implode his hastily constructed redoubt.

"What do you mean before I get my defenses up? They're always up because of you. I've never been able to completely trust another man, thanks to you. I loved you, and you knew it. I gave you all the love I had, and how did you respond? By breaking up with me. All because you'd been with Shelly and, and—" Her voice broke. "Well, Veronica says it all, doesn't she?"

"Jane—" Cord barely got his word out when the cannons exploded again.

"My parents wouldn't let me stay out graduation night, so you had to find someone else to be with. That really showed how much you cared about me. One night was too much for you to wait. I'm sure Shelly was more than happy to take care of your needs." The glass in Jane's hand was shaking again, and as she used it to emphasize her points, the level of the liquid sank lower and lower, the wood under her feet glistening in the flickering candlelight.

"Then, you didn't even tell me about it until weeks later when you broke up with me. That was the part that hurt most." Her voice was crushed, as if something had broken inside, and her next words were little more than a quivering whisper. "I trusted you. I could have forgiven you almost anything. But to get a phone call from the one person I loved and trusted, and to be told that it was over? No, I'll never be able to let my defenses down. Not now. Not ever."

She turned away, her cheeks glistening.

"Mi corazón," Cord began, his voice thick with emotion. "You don't understand." He stepped to her, hesitant. He wanted to touch her, to hold her hand. If he could touch her, she'd feel how much he loved her, had always loved her, even though forty years had been stolen from them. And they had been stolen. He hadn't known that then, not at the beginning. But they'd been stolen, and he wanted back what he could get.

Even if it was just for Jane to understand.

"I had to tell you over the phone. I knew I'd never be able to do it face to face. I loved you too much."

"You loved me and couldn't tell me to my face that you were marrying another woman? I don't think so, Cord." Tears continued to stream down her face. "You don't love a person, not the way I loved you, and twist the knife you've thrust into their heart. It just doesn't work that way."

"Oh, mi corazón." He'd known even then what he was doing to her, and his hands had been tied. He'd had no choice, and now he'd brought it all back again. "Jane, mi corazón, I wouldn't have hurt you. I couldn't face you, not and move on. I had no choice."

"I had only—" Her voice broke. "You, Cord. I only loved you, and only that once—"

"That once." He took a deep breath. "I've held that in my thoughts as the most precious memory I own. No matter what I did, the abuse Shelly threw at me, I held to our memory. That night was the only thing that kept me going."

"Then why?" She turned to him, her voice soft, the anger melted, the pleading telling of the pain inside.

"The truth." He couldn't say . . . didn't want to say . . . mustn't sully Veronica's birth. His daughter . . . he loved her, and she was his as much as any child could be. "I want you to believe me more than anything, Jane. I really do. But nothing I say will convince you of the truth. I see that now. You no longer trust me." If he told the truth . . . and yet he bit his words back.

"I want to trust you," she whispered. "I want more than anything to believe everything you say and trust everything you do." She put her hand out as if to rest it on his chest, then, at the last moment, she turned it and wiped the tears from her face. "You hurt me too deeply. Then you sit here and tell me you were never with Shelly. Your daughter tells the truth. You can't deny her."

"That night, Jane, graduation night." He felt the words flooding forth, the dam broken, and he could no longer contain the breach. "I so wanted you there. The guys, first they spiked the punch, and there were bottles everywhere. One went in my hand, and I don't know why I did it. Then there was another, and I stumbled off into the darkness. Dear God, how did I let that happen?" He put his hand to his face, covering his eyes, to regain control.

"Let what happen, Cord?" Her voice was calmer, as if maybe this was what she'd wanted after all.

"I don't know what happened. I guess I passed out, and when I woke, Shelly was lying beside me telling me how much fun she'd had."

"Fun?" There was no sharpness in Jane's question, just pleading for an explanation.

"She was," and he rubbed his hand over his head, "and I cringe when I say this, in her, you know, skivvies. And my shoes were off." He grimaced. "Honestly, Jane, I didn't remember anything. Not a thing."

"But yet she said . . ."

Cord nodded.

"And you . . ."

"There's something else you might want to know. It might make a difference to you." He hadn't wanted to make this part of his plea for clemency, but he was desperate. "Veronica's birthday is—"

Cord didn't get to finish. Just then the lights flickered once, and with the gentle whirring of the refrigerator in the kitchen and the low whoosh of air from the vents, the lights came on and stayed. Somewhere in the background something beeped three times, possibly the smoke detectors or the phones.

Jane's face hardened, and the mood for sharing was over.

— 19 —

"I THINK IT'S TIME I got back to the guesthouse. There are still a lot of things I need to finish up before the reunion party this weekend."

Jane had listened to all she could stand. Cord might not have ruined her life on purpose, but ruined was ruined. And who cared when Veronica's birthday was? Good grief! If only that man knew how badly her life had been devastated. Forgive? She was prepared to do that. Forget? This would always be between them like a heavy curtain, their hearts never quite able to reach each other's.

She needed trust. Love? She had loved Cord, and she could easily do so again. But trust . . . that's what true love was, trust. And that was the one thing she no longer had in Cord. Trust. She couldn't believe in him as much as she needed to allow love into the picture.

But she could finish this house, and that she would do.

"Jane?"

She turned. "You're not finished, yet? Okay, what?" She was out of patience with this tonight.

"Are you sure you wouldn't rather stay in here out of the weather? You can have my room, and I'll be comfortable right here on the sofa."

"We've already discussed this. Why are you still asking me this?" Her voice was sharper than she intended, but it seemed appropriate. They had discussed it, and she had declined. Did he think something so silly would soften her resolve?

"The rain . . ." He smiled. "It's still coming down in sheets."

"In sheets?" Ten minutes ago, she could have laughed at the double entendre. No longer. "I was having a pleasant time with you, and you took a twenty-two and fired a whole load of buckshot into my balloon. I think the guesthouse is just where I need to be. My little casita for the week will do me just fine for the night. However, I'll be out tomorrow." There was no way she was staying another night. No way.

"No!" Cord's reply was edged with steel.

"No?" She raised her eyebrows.

"I'm a gentleman, no matter what you may think of me. At least I must escort you to your door in this weather." Cord spoke in his rich, honeyed voice, yet there was something else there, a new determination.

Jane was surprised to see him grab an umbrella and head toward the back door. She was even more surprised for him to do it with her under his arm. What surprised her most of all was that she offered no protest to his proffered help.

With one hand on the umbrella and the other tightly holding her waist, he safely delivered her to the guest cabana porch. Jane mumbled a good night as she unlocked the door and hurried through it.

Inside, she leaned against the door and let out a deep breath. She was older than she'd been all those years ago, but was she any wiser? It was the thrumming in her wrists and in her neck that told her the truth. It was her heart upside down, and her thoughts in a muddle that screamed at her, telling her that if she stayed here even tonight, she was a sucker, and she would fall for Cord once again, hook, line, and sinker, just as she had all those years ago.

Moving away from the door, Jane sat on the edge of the bed, reaching to turn on the fan sitting on the bedside table. The storm had cooled the air outside, but it was still muggy in her quarters. With a quick twist, she dropped her hair around her shoulders, shaking it free. She wished it was so easy to unknot this problem with Cord, just shaking him out of her hair as easily as one, two, three.

It was working off her makeup that brought her true feelings home. Rubbing the cream into her skin and wiping it away, she caught her eyes in the mirror. They were red and shimmering with moisture. She knew what from, too.

She loved Cord. She'd never stopped loving him, even when she'd felt the most betrayed. She'd just never understood, and eventually, she'd been forced to put it all behind her.

Well, it wasn't behind her, now. It was right out in front, talking to her, taking her to dinner, and letting her design his home and all the furnishings.

"Ooh!" She growled. "Satan, get thee behind me."

But the words that kept going through her head haunted her. *Forgive. Forget. Don't be angry. Love.*

"Ooh!" She growled again. This time she didn't do more, because she knew who those words were from. And she'd better do what He said. After all, it wasn't like He was giving her a choice.

"Ooh!" She growled again.

— 20 —

IT WAS THE SUN in her face that awakened Jane. She turned her head to bury her face in the pillow, only to find it damp with last night's tears. That was the final straw, and she knew she couldn't remain in her bed one more minute.

Besides, blowup mattresses simply did not do for her back what her down-filled one did at home.

Throwing back the covers and standing, she glanced around the room. It was ... different. She stood, thinking, very puzzled as the dappled light flickered and shifted around her. Then the room darkened as a cloud covered the sun, and just as quickly, the light scattered across the floor like a handful of diamonds cast carelessly across the wooden surface.

Then it hit her. Trees! The landscapers had managed to get the ornamental trees in before the weather had turned yesterday. She pulled her pajamas around her and stepped to the wall of casement windows fronting the pool area. Hanging baskets filled with flowers of bright pinks, oranges, and reds hung throughout the patio area, making it look like an old, well-maintained Spanish garden on some king's country estate. She smiled. It was as beautiful as she'd pictured it that first day here with Cord, and even more beautiful than it had been when she had first visited here all those decades ago. Good! The old place had needed this, and she was pleased.

Then something else hit her. Last night. Cord, in the house, and his words to her. His lies to her. She looked back into the room, looking at the things she'd collected here, how in just a few days, it had taken on a feeling of home. It was just a blow-up mattress—even if a very elaborate and expensive one—and a chair from the new dining room furniture. That and an old console, one that she remembered from Cord's parents' days. It had been in the attic, dusty, but in very serviceable condition. She had brought it down and cleaned it one evening after the house had gone dark. She wondered if Cord would want it in the house, or if he would sell it to her. It was good quality, and she would pay whatever he asked.

Pay whatever he asked. Humph! It was just a drop of what she was charging him, no matter how much he asked. Maybe it was too much to ask for the console. Besides, it would remind her of Cord. Just the thought of that brought a knot to her stomach.

Rummaging in her bag, she pulled out some personals, and in the small closet, she found a lightweight blouse, teal with gold threading, and tan slacks. Stepping into the bathroom, she ran a brush through her hair and dressed. She peered into the mirror, deciding on whether makeup was called for. This was to be a working day. Working and packing. She wasn't staying another day. She'd made that very clear to Cord.

She took a deep breath. Last day. Back in the Lexus, which she hadn't driven in almost a week. Bill's last gift to her. God knew she could afford a new one on her own. The business was making money hand over fist, especially on this job. Still, it was Bill's last gift, and it had almost no miles on it.

It was the tears that decided her. Sunglasses and a wide-brimmed hat would do the trick. Makeup would run, and with last night's rain and today's sun, the humidity would be unbearable, she was certain. And this room would become a hothouse. It would be nice to get back to her own place, with its air-conditioned comfort and feather mattress.

Stepping outside, the scent of the crape myrtles assailed her. Along with the palms, bougainvillea, and climbing roses, the yard was perfection. Now all the landscapers had to do was clear the patio areas and edge the new grass plantings.

The rain had been better for the landscape than any irrigation system ever could be. She'd have to make sure the underground piping was disengaged for the day so as not to flood the plantings. Note one, she tagged in her head. But it was time for her to gather her things and go home. Home . . . she felt neither the urge to go back nor homesickness to see it. To be honest, she hadn't missed her home in the time she'd stayed here.

When she turned, she saw the note attached beside the door. *In town. See you when I return.* That's all, and in Cord's handwriting. Good. This was her chance to be gone before he returned. Seeing him? That was a two-edged sword, one that cut with love and betrayal. She didn't need that sword anywhere near her. The quicker she loaded her things, the better her day would be.

AS SHE WAS PREPARING to go back for her sewing machine, Jane heard Cord's vehicle coming up the driveway. He honked and motioned for her to stop.

"What are you doing?" He motioned to her suitcase and make-up bag at the back of her car. "Surely you weren't leaving until I gave my final approval?"

Final approval? She felt her tears rise, and she was glad for the sunglasses. Her escape hadn't been quick enough, and she didn't know if she could survive the thrust of the knife one more time. Not after last night.

"My number hasn't changed. It's on the contract if you need to call." She waved and smiled, good at her public presentation. After all, she was Jane Waggoner, designer, and she did work for very influential and important people. She did know how to grease the bumps out of her day. She had to, to survive.

"You can't meet my favorite girl over the phone." He grinned. "She's the new love of my life. I was in town to pick her up at the bus station, but you know how it is." He opened his door and climbed out, motioning to show there was no one with him.

"No, I don't know how it is. Why don't you tell me?" The love of his life? Suddenly, everything was clear. Jane's face was tight, and she could feel her eyes burn. She didn't want to cry, not today, not in front of this man. *Dear God*, she prayed, *I don't want to cry.*

In contrast, Cord seemed very pleased with himself. "Of course, the bus is running late. By several hours, too. Traffic on 20 was stalled for hours by an overturned semi. The desk said by noon, maybe. They'll give me a call since I have to drive back in. You'll still be here then?" Cord finished with a grin on his face. He seemed truly excited about Jane meeting the new love in his life.

Jane barely heard his words. How could she have been so stupid? Of course, he was doing this for someone else, not just himself. He'd planned this all along. He'd used his charm and their old connection to get her to do the very best designs and decorations for his house, and all for someone else, someone who wanted to live in this grand old place, who would cook at the granite counters, wash her hands using the water heater she'd worked so hard to put in, and probably tear out her shell soap holders in the guest bath simply because she liked ceramic flowers better. Ceramic flowers didn't even match Spanish hacienda style!

"No, I believe I'll pass up the honor." Jane made sure her words were carefully modulated. She wanted none of her pain and disappointment to bleed through. She also wanted nothing to do with meeting this other woman. It might be fine for Cord and Veronica to invite a new woman into the household, but she didn't want anything to do with it. She ignored the disappointment on Cord's face. Instead, she pointed to the door of the guesthouse. "If you don't mind, would you please bring my sewing machine from the guesthouse, and I'll be on my way. We'll wrap up the final details by the weekend."

"But aren't your son and his family coming by before the reunion?" Cord's eyes twinkled.

"Billy?" She had forgotten.

"You have another son, or is it perhaps a daughter you haven't told me about?" He seemed amused.

"No." She temporized. "I was planning to, um, sort out the final paperwork and bring the closing statements by, and Saturday will be fine." She nodded briskly, adjusting the sunglasses on her face. With her hat, she didn't really need the glasses, but with her heart, they were proving indispensable.

"Good. You can meet Vangie then. Well, Evangeline, actually. Veronica liked her the first time she met her. They've become good friends over the past few weeks." He laughed. "Veronica thinks you'll like her, too."

That was the final straw, that Cord's daughter thought Jane and his new wife would want to be friends. No, she could wait a lifetime before letting that happen. She was finished with Juan Cordello Rivera the Third.

It was when he stepped to get her sewing machine that he stopped, transfixed. He turned to her. "It was dark when I left this morning. I didn't see all this. Jane, you're the most remarkably talented woman I've ever known. I consider it both a privilege and an honor for you to have designed and decorated both my home and surrounding yard area. I'm blessed to have you in my life."

That knocked the skids from under her. A new woman in his life, and now he was telling her with tears in his eyes how grateful he was to have her in his life as well? That was more than she could handle.

"Well, thank you, but you may not think I'm so great after seeing my final bill. I really do need to go now, and if I've forgotten something, I'll get it later." With the sewing machine forgotten, Jane turned and climbed into her car, careful not to look at Cord. She was afraid he might see the truth in her face, the truth that he had once again broken her heart.

This time it was for good.

— 21 —

JANE HAD NO SOONER left Cord's driveway than a torrent of tears flooded her face. She'd been wrong all along. She hadn't been reading his signals correctly. Now, here she was again with another broken heart.

But this time she had only herself to blame.

She had thought, perhaps hoped at one point, that she and Cord could repair the damaged tapestry in which their history had entangled them. The trust could be rebuilt; the love could regrow. Even the lie from last night. She'd been furious, but that now paled with the news from this morning.

"Ooh!" She wiped the tears from her face, flinging the sunglasses aside when they got in her way. "God, why? How can you let me be so stupid?"

It was those messages from her devotional. She'd begun to trust them. She'd begun to trust in God that He would work this out, that the past could be mended if she simply trusted in Him.

Apparently, Cord didn't share the same feelings for her. To make matters worse, he had a new love. For a while she had thought, or perhaps hoped that he had wanted her and his daughter to be close. It seemed she was wrong on that account as well. Veronica was keeping company with "Vangie."

Why hadn't she been able to read the signs? Yes, he'd been away from the hacienda a lot lately, but she assumed it was because of his job. It never occurred to her that he might be seeing someone else.

And taking her to dinner last night? What was that about, nothing more than a final evening to wind up a job that was in its closing hours? Was she a pariah, someone to be used and cast aside? Was that the lesson Cord had learned from their relationship so many years ago?

Her tears had slowed to a trickle by the time she got home. She let herself into the house and collapsed on her sofa, exhausted from her emotional roller coaster. Her body felt like lead weights had been added to it, and it refused to move. Even when the phone rang, she didn't have the energy to answer. Right then, she didn't care who was on the other line. She couldn't. Even her "line" to God had turned out to be a misleading series of road signs that she had misinterpreted and gone back to again and again to convince herself that an old relationship could be renewed if only she gave in on all her principles.

She curled her legs on the sofa, laying her head on the arm, and closing her eyes. It wasn't more than a few minutes of lying there before she admitted her bed was a better option, no matter how much effort it took. Brushing her teeth, she thought of Cord, that night she'd hurt her ankle. He'd been so kind, here to see that she was taken care of. Bill had never done that for her, not waited on her hand and foot. She guessed she'd let her need for what Cord had seemed to offer blind her to the truth. In forty years, he'd built a life for himself, and it hadn't included her.

Now she had nothing, not the small hope she'd carried underneath all her hurt and pain that Cord somehow still cared, nor Billy, that small boy that had filled the emptiness that had ripped her world apart. She was totally alone as she crawled into her oversized bed, that great envelope of comfortable luxury made for two that now cradled only her.

Her dreams were of a pleasanter time, of school days, those before college or the heartbreak of the year after Cord left her. She dreamed of an old Ford pickup with running boards on the side, a radio that only got five stations and an 8-track player that skipped every time Cord tore over the railroad tracks without slowing down.

In that world she sat at a table in the Dairy Queen, the real one that was gone now, and she was with her friends admiring a long-legged boy in a tight tee shirt, round-toe boots, and faded jeans. It was the first time he'd looked at her, and she'd glanced away, embarrassed. He was Juan Cordello Rivera, his family was the richest in town, and there was no way he was interested in her. Not like that.

He had been, though. Of all the girls in the school, Tarzan had chased her, and she'd run, but not for long, becoming the Jane to his Tarzan.

In her dream, as dreams will do, the Dairy Queen was deep in the wildest jungle. Outside wandered elephants, tigers, and chimpanzees. One of the chimps kept tapping on the window at Jane's side, distracting her. Finally, she turned to it, irritated, and she said loudly, "What?"

The chimpanzee started making hand signs at her, pointing first to Cord, then to Jane. Jane realized it was sign language, and she frowned as she watched the big, bulky chimp fingers form the words.

It was odd, too, because the chimp formed Tarzan, then Jane, but it was the last word, the name for itself that seemed to give it trouble.

"Cheetah?" Jane called the name helpfully, hoping the poor creature could hear her. Instead, the animal shook its head. It was only after several starts and stops that Jane pronounced the words the finger seemed to spell. "Peg Tee?" The chimp pounded on the window, hooting, and tried again.

Then, Jane laughed. "Peggy! But she's right here." She turned to her side to see that there was no one next to her. "You?" She pointed to the glass.

"You're Peggy?" The chimp slapped itself on the chest in affirmation.

Jane laughed. In her dream, she laughed and laughed. It was the best time of her life, and it was all back again. Then, the phone rang and pulled her into the real world once again.

"Hello, yes, I'm awake now." Jane spoke sharply into the telephone, not really awake at all.

"Oh, well, that was some greeting." It was Peggy on the other end.

"Oh, it's you." Jane fell back onto her pillow. "I was resting. I think you woke me."

"I'm sure. It's about time. I just got back from supper." She sounded very pleased with herself.

"Supper?" Jane pulled the clock from the bedside table. "It's only ten."

"In the evening. Have you been asleep all day? I haven't been able to get through to you, and I've called a lot."

"I had a bad night last night—"

"All that lightning. Me, too. I didn't sleep a wink."

"So, what did you have for supper?" She closed her eyes, allowing Peggy to talk away. She usually did, so this should be an easy conversation. Jane was willing to let Peggy think it was the lightning that had disturbed her sleep, but then maybe it was. The lightning in her heart. The other kind? That didn't bother her much.

"Well, Cord called me, and Vangie's in town. I'm

so excited. I couldn't talk about her before, but now that Cord's told you about her, well, that means all holds are off. I mean, she's the sweetest thing, and she really wants to get to know you." Peggy giggled, her enthusiasm bleeding over the phone line.

"Whoa, Peggy. Yes, I got Cord's *news*, if you want to call it that, and while he told me enough, it wasn't all that much. Right now, I don't want to hear any more, thank you." Jane was wide-awake now. How could Peggy do this to her? It was the ultimate betrayal, her best friend meeting and having dinner with the new love in Cord's life. Then she had the nerve to call her and tell her about it. What kind of friend was she? Obviously, a fair-weather one, at best.

"I tried to call you all afternoon to tell you about it, so don't blame me. You never answered your phone. I thought perhaps you were going to be at the hacienda, too. But when I arrived, Cord explained how you seemed distracted when you left, so I didn't call you again. Vangie is so sweet. You're going to love her—"

Jane interrupted Peggy from going on any further. "If you would, kindly remember to whom you are talking. I never want to meet or talk about Vangie. I haven't met her, and I'm already sick of her and her syrupy name."

"But, Jane—"

Peggy barely got the words out before Jane lit into her again. "If you were really my friend, you'd have refused the invitation and would never speak to Cord again. He's hurt me so deeply by throwing this other woman up in my face. He told me he wanted me to meet the new love in his life. I've never been so crushed or devastated ever!" Jane's voice broke over the phone, and she hung up.

Her face hot and her eyes burning, she threw the bedding back and stumbled into the bathroom, flipping the shower on high. She needed to wash everything away. Yesterday, and now Peggy's words, clung to her like old sweat, and she could smell it on herself. What was it about her that Cord didn't seem to care about? What could she do to make Cord ever want her?

Of course, it didn't matter now, because he'd found someone new to love. That was the hardest part, knowing he'd forgotten how much they'd once loved each other.

At least he didn't hate her. If he knew the whole truth, he might feel differently, and that would be even worse. She preferred his indifference to his hate any day.

— 22 —

JANE LOOKED AT THE sign just in front of her. Bladell's Department Store. If Cord liked flashy women, then she would prove a point to him, and Bladell's was just the place. They knew flashy, if anyone did.

She flipped the mirror down and studied herself in the reflection. Extra lipstick? Check. Mascara to make a man cry? Check. Seamless perfection? Check. She smiled as she opened the car, careful not to smile too widely so as not to crack the perfection. She was going for the gold, and that meant taking a risk. Getting the gold meant perfection, and she was up for it, including wearing the slinkiest outfit she owned.

This was her fallback plan. She admitted that. It was only fair to do so. She had loved Bill, but he'd been a stand in for the man she'd lost. At first, at least. God knew she had hated herself for that, but what was done was done. She'd been faithful to Bill, a good wife, and a committed Christian all those years, eventually coming to appreciate his stability and caring, if distant, concern. Nothing was going to change that, either. But Bill had abandoned her three years before, even if not by his choice. Still, abandonment was abandonment. Then Cord had shown up six weeks ago, with all his charm and good looks, and as much as she'd railed against all the memories, she'd been attracted to him. It was high school all over.

Now she felt dumped as cruelly as before, only this time she wasn't taking it on the chin. She was fighting back. Even if Cord had another woman under his wing, there were a couple of widowers and three or four divorced men in her class who might possibly show up at the reunion. Who was to say she might not wow one of them? It was time she got back into the game of life. Peggy was right. She couldn't be the grieving widow forever.

She breezed into the store, exuding confidence and bravado, she hoped. She had to. This was a store for the elite, and anything she bought here would eat up a big chunk of Cord's change.

Of course, it was money she'd earned, but it would come from Cord's pocket, and somehow that seemed very satisfying.

A sales associate helped her select three possible

contenders. The first had a plunging neckline and tucked tightly at the waist. The waist was good. The neckline? She didn't know if she wanted to be *that* flashy. The second . . . backless? Surely not, she easily decided. The full skirt—diaphanous—would catch in the slightest breeze. She shivered at that thought. It was the third that caught her eye. Rich blue and yellow sequins on a strapless, satin band over a fitted, soft yellow bodice. The skirt had a short slit up the side. She loved it! A minor adjustment to the hem, which she could do in a heartbeat, and it would be perfect.

Bladell's even carried shoes to match.

She couldn't wait to show it off to Billy and Jasmine when they came in. Not too daring, but certainly different than anyone would expect from her. The men at the reunion—she blocked the thought of Cord from her mind—would be wowed.

New earrings in blue and yellow would set off her fresh outfit perfectly, and she was so lucky to have an account at J. Gale's across the street. Today was coming together perfectly.

When she stepped out of the store, she laid her new outfit in the truck of her car and stepped to the curb to cross the street. That was when she saw the black truck parked right in front of J. Gale's.

Cord.

"What's he doing here?" She muttered her comment, and then it hit her. He was parked at the jewelers.

"Probably buying Vangie a ring. Engagement, unless I miss my guess."

Suddenly she didn't feel the need to shop for earrings. Her stomach twisted, and she wanted to be away, back in the safety of her home, and out of public view. She felt silly with her heavy makeup—no longer perfect, but a desperate old woman out on the prowl.

Oh, she hated this.

She whipped around, striding to her car with as much grace and aplomb as she could muster in her desperation. Before she could shut her door, she heard a whistle and her name.

"Hey, Jane! Is that you?"

No! He couldn't see her here! "No, it only looks like me!" She didn't say that, but heavens knew she thought about it. Instead, she waved and tried to duck into her car. She almost made it before a hand caught the door and pulled it wide.

"Oh, you are beautiful today."

He was panting. He must have run across the street. Even that irritated her.

"Thank you," *as you buy a ring for your new honey. How's this like forty years ago? Exactly, that's how.* "You look nice, too."

He was in dark jeans, with pointed boots, and a tailored black shirt. He looked more than good, but Jane wasn't admitting that to him.

"Is this what you're wearing to the reunion?" He seemed extraordinarily pleased with himself.

"No, Cord. This is just an old thing I threw on. My new dress is in the trunk." She put her hand to her face, feeling the warmth build. What was with her? She was being mean and spiteful, not Christian at all.

"Well, whatever it is, I know you'll look great in it. You have such beautiful taste."

"Um, thank you, I guess." Now she was flustered. Compliments? Was he interested? And, of all things, where was his "Vangie" woman? Ooh, things were not making sense to her. "So, what are you doing in town today?" As if he had to explain to her.

"I had to get a few last-minute details taken care of before tomorrow. Veronica and the kids came down late last evening, and they're with Vangie shopping for the reunion. You'd think they've known each other all their lives." He chuckled, and it was deep and resonant.

Jane had no desire to hear about Vangie and how she fit so neatly into the lives of Cord's family members. "Well, that's great and all, but I need to get home. Peggy and I have some plans of our own."

It was a bald-faced lie, but she couldn't help it. She couldn't let him see how desperately she still cared about him, and how he was torturing her each time he mentioned Vangie's name.

"I understand. She'll be out of her pottery class soon, so I won't keep you. I'll see you tomorrow at the hacienda." With that, Cord bent down and kissed Jane's forehead and shut her door.

Jane watched him walk away, and she was dazed.

Now she was more confused than ever. With her eyes burning and her nerves shattered, she pulled her phone from her clutch, punching in Peggy's number.

"Peggy, you will not believe . . ." She poured out the entire morning on her friend's shoulders. She wasn't prepared for Peggy's response.

"You've got to start trusting again, Jane. The world isn't your enemy, and neither is Cord. If you'd just try to trust and believe in him, I know you'd see things differently."

"That's easy for you to say. You weren't hurt by him like I was." She was not going to let Peggy off that easily.

"I know he hurt you back in high school. Everyone in town knows that. We all expected you two to get married. But it didn't end up that way. Now he wants to make amends, and you won't even try to trust him."

"What's the point, now? He's already found someone new. He told me with his own mouth he has a new love. And you even went over and had dinner with them." Jane had called for her friend's support, not to have her knees cut from under her. She knew her words sounded hurt and angry, but she felt hurt and angry. She couldn't pretend any other way, not after what had just happened.

"Yes, and I thought you might have been there, too. I expected to see you. But since you refuse to even meet him halfway, I'm glad he has someone who does love him without huge expectations of what he should and shouldn't be. I'm sorry, Jane. Class just let out, and I must get to my hair appointment. Just think about it, though." Without so much as a by-your-leave, the phone went dead.

Jane held up her phone and looked at it. She couldn't believe Peggy. She wanted her to trust Cord again. And she was glad Cord had Vangie? Ooh!

Well, she had a dress to alter, and she planned to bedazzle all those old men and women at the reunion tomorrow. She would be the glittering belle of the ball, and no one would be able to hold a candle to her.

She even tried to push away the words that hovered in the back of her mind. *Forgive. Forget. Don't be angry. Love.* It was the "don't be angry" part that goaded her today. How could she not be angry? Everything had gone wrong, and now even her best friend had abandoned her.

When she pulled out of the parking lot, she was surprised to see Cord's truck pulling out across from her. He rolled his window down and waved, as if she was a good friend, and there was nothing in the world to drive them apart.

Except Vangie, Jane thought. You have another woman, Cord, and that'll keep us as far apart as the east is from the west.

That phrase reminded her of her Sunday school lesson the week before, and she felt a twinge of guilt. That was how far God threw our sins when we repented, and he never remembered them again. That story reminded her of something else.

Forgive. Forget. Don't be angry. Love.

"Ooh!" she growled for the umpteenth time, even as she knew God was right. She had to do it all, and it was going to be the toughest thing she'd ever done.

— 23 —

"BILLY, COME GIVE me a hug." Jane left the front door ajar and held out her arms. They had just driven up, and her stepson's car door was open.

"Hello, Mom." Jasmine waved from the other side of the car. "The kids are wrapping up their movie. They'll be out in a few minutes."

"It's so nice to see you, Jasmine. How was the drive?"

"Mom? A new diet?" It was Billy that responded. He grinned.

"Oh, don't listen to him," interjected Jasmine. "He wouldn't know a diet if he saw one. You look fabulous. You've let your hair grow out some, and I like this softer style. I thought it was too short before, but it was none of my business. However, it looks so good now, I have to say something."

By that time Jane had her arms around Billy. She glanced in the car to see the kids huddled in front of a portable DVD player. She was just glad for the distraction. Bladell's? That had about done her in.

"New car, Billy?" It was blue, and Jane remembered a green one.

"Just picked it up last week. American made, a Cadillac. XTS." He stroked one fender. "Jasmine keeps it home for errands."

"It's very pretty. Kids? Coming in?" She leaned in through the front door. "Little Billy? Katherine?"

"Hi, Grandma," they chorused, their eyes never leaving the screen.

"Kids!" Jasmine laughed, leaning over and giving Jane a kiss on the cheek. "Thirteen and fifteen, and they still love a good video. Leave them be. At least they're occupied quietly."

She was right, too. The backseat was evidence of that. Popcorn was everywhere, with books, scattered game pieces, and candy wrappers. Jane knew they'd leave her house in about the same condition, if they got a chance.

"Well, I have dinner ready, and they can eat it cold if they're not hungry. How about you and Billy?" He was at the back of the car unloading suitcases.

"You fix it, and Billy will come." Jasmine put her arm in Jane's, walking toward the door. "Now, tell me about this ranch you've been redoing. I want to hear every detail, from the kitchen sink to the bathroom soap holders."

"Oh, you don't want to hear about the soap holders." Jane remembered her rant about those, and she smiled.

"Oh?"

"I think the owner has plans to tear them out as soon as he pays me for putting them in." She giggled, knowing it was silly. "Not really, but you never know. I learned yesterday the ranch's owner has a new fiancée."

"No!"

"He's been redoing the house for her."

"He told you that?" Billy was right behind them with a suitcase in each hand.

"Not in so many words. Billy, you should let Little Billy get those for you." They were inside, and she watched him maneuver them through the door.

"I'm sure he would, if I didn't care whether they made it in tonight or in the morning. I care." He dropped them by the front door. "Did I hear something about food?" He took a sniff and smiled.

"On the stove just waiting for four hungry mouths."

"Will two do?" He grinned.

"Make it three. I'm hungry, too." Jane led the way, waving her family along after her. The food would have drawn them the direction of the kitchen, anyway. Roast and potatoes could pull anyone in.

THE KIDS HAD JOINED them, their plates piled high, and they were finishing cake and ice cream, when the phone rang.

"I've got it. You go ahead." Jane stood and slipped her cell phone from the counter. "Yes?"

"Who is it, Mom?" Billy had cake on his fork, and he tucked it into his mouth.

"Your Aunt Peggy, I think." She took a deep breath, refusing to let her stepson know how irritated she'd been with her earlier. After a moment she said, "They're here now. Come on over."

Jasmine looked puzzled. "I've never figured out how Peggy is Billy's aunt. Is she a great-aunt, once removed, or . . ." She held out her hand, palm up, as if waiting on an explanation.

"Neither." Billy was scooping another spoonful of ice cream from the bucket. "Right, Mom?"

"Aunt Peggy's not our aunt?" Little Billy asked around his latest bite.

His sister hit him on the arm. "Is, too. Right, Grandma?"

"She might as well be." Jane returned the phone to the counter. Peggy was as close to a sister as she'd ever have. For that reason, she'd better let her irritation go. She smiled. "She's your aunt—" and she pointed her finger at Katherine "—just not by blood."

"She's a love aunt?" Little Billy grinned, jabbing his sister in the side with his elbow.

"Stop that," Jasmine said, rapping the table. "You two want to be rowdy, you go in the back yard. You can be rowdy tunes as much as you want out there."

"Okay." Little Billy leaped up. "Rowdy tunes. You're it." He punched his sister on the shoulder, and leaving his chair out, he ran for the back door.

"No fair, Mom. I didn't know he was playing." Katherine sat with a pained expression on her face.

"You know now." That was Billy. "Go get him."

"Okay." Her face brightened. "Can I take a roll?"

Jane held the plate to her, smiling when the girl took two and ran after her brother.

"Bet you're glad you only had me." Billy grinned.

Jane wasn't, though. She'd always wanted more. A daughter. Her daughter. Just one more would have done her fine. That hadn't been the way it had worked out, though.

The doorbell rang, and Jane called out, "It's open."

Jasmine raised her eyebrows.

Billy coughed, "Mom?"

Jane wrinkled her nose. "It's just Peggy. Don't worry about her. She knows her way in the house." As well as out, but that didn't need said.

"Well, how's Jane's favorite little man?" Peggy flew into the room, giving him a hug.

"Not so little." Jasmine reached and patted his waistline.

"Embarrassed." Billy dropped his head, grinning. "Can't I be just Billy?"

"I've greeted you that way for nearly forty years, and I'm not changing now." She turned to Jane. "And you?" She made a sour face. "You done any thinking?"

"Let it go, Peggy. Talk to your nephew."

"How are you, Aunt Peggy? What's been keeping you busy?"

"You know us old hippies; we still do what we like to do. Pottery. Jewelry. Like always. My design classes are going great. I haven't seen my own children since Christmas, but they call about every two weeks or a month, and we play catch-up."

"Not very maternal, are you?" Jane was quite aware she hadn't managed to let all her irritation slip away.

"Well, I'm here, and they're the ones that decided to move away. I couldn't very well chase them down and lasso them back." She smiled sweetly. "Where are the kids? That little Katherine was so sweet last time you were here. I swear she's the image of her mother."

"Out back, being very much *not* like her mother." Jasmine smiled ruefully. "Her mother is better behaved." Billy shot her a look, and she slapped him on the arm. "Not a word, buster."

Peggy laughed. "Peas in a pod. You just can't tell, Jasmine. Are you bringing them to the reunion tomorrow?"

"We'll see when the time comes. Right now, I think we all need to burn some energy." Billy motioned to the back yard, where the children could be heard involved in a fracas.

"Well, I want to remember them as sweet, so I had better go. I still have a few more things to do before the big day. So until then, have a good evening!" Peggy said her good-byes, blew kisses to everyone, and left.

"Dears," Jane said, standing, "you can leave all this, but I do think I'll lie down for a time. Last night was a long one."

"Mom, you're not still having nightmares about Dad's death are you?" Billy put his fork down and looked at her, really looked for the first time.

"No, sweetie, those stopped some months back, but the new one is just about as bad." Cord, but that wasn't her stepson's problem.

"What's it, now?"

"Your mother said she could handle it. Let her be." Jasmine patted his arm.

"She's right. It's really nothing I can't handle. I'm just glad all my babies are here. I think I sleep better when I know you're close by. And no, that's not a hint for you to move here. I'm thinking about coming up there for a few weeks if you think you can stand me for that long."

Billy looked over at Jasmine, who smiled wide. "You just like her to do all the cooking."

"Shush, you big baby. Of course, I do. Tell her we accept."

"Sure, Mom. That would be great. You know we always love it when you visit. Just tell us when, and we'll have the guest room ready." Billy grinned, glancing at his wife.

"It might be sooner than you think."

"Anytime, Mom. Anytime." Billy gave Jane a little pat on her arm.

"Yes, anytime, Mom." Jasmine echoed her husband's words.

Jane retired to her room, not really expecting to get much rest. Peggy had thrown her for yet another loop. *You done any thinking?* She knew what she meant. However, what good did it do? Cord had Vangie, life had ended forty years ago, and all she had was an incredibly expensive dress in the back of her car.

That stopped her short. The dress was still in the trunk, and the car was in the garage.

Ooh! When would she ever get a grip on life? Like, never?

Ooh!

— 24 —

"HOW DO I LOOK?"

"Mom! Look at you!"

Jane turned around, letting her stepson take in her new dress. "Do you think I got it too short?"

"Absolutely not. You'll wow everyone there this evening." He called, "Jasmine, you've got to come see this."

"Ooh, la, la." Jasmine stepped in, still running a brush through her hair. "I should look so good at thir-ty-five."

Jane felt her face warm. "Do you really think so? Not too showy?" Her nerves were getting the better of her, and she thought perhaps she had gone a little too far in her attempt to get even with Cord for breaking her heart.

"Are you kidding, Mom? You look fabulous, and I mean it. You'll be the belle of the ball tonight at the reunion. Don't change a thing. I hope I look half as good as you when I reach your age," Jasmine finished her compliments and gave Jane's arm a good squeeze. "Don't worry about Billy. He's just not used to seeing you as anything but his mom," Jasmine whispered in her ear.

Jane stepped to the mirror in the front hall, evaluating herself. Her hair, full and with soft curls, hung just to her chin. Her new hemline cut at her knees, and the satin band with all its sequins glittered.

"Here, Mom." Jasmine stepped to her and held out her hand. "Try these." Inside were two yellow diamond earrings.

"These are beautiful. Wherever did you get them?"

"Billy." She leaned against him and patted his chest. "For our fifteenth anniversary. But tonight, they're yours. The color . . . when I saw your dress, I knew you had to have these on."

"How could I be so lucky to have such a wonderful daughter-in-law?" Jane felt her eyes fill up, and she grabbed Jasmine by the shoulders and gently brushed her cheek with a kiss. "You, Billy, have exquisite taste." She patted his cheek with her hand.

"For the diamonds?" He grinned.

"For the girl." Jane nodded, slipping her gold studs out to make room for the diamonds.

Jasmine grinned.

"Are the kids ready?" Jane thought not, not with the ruckus from down the hall, but she hoped the question would get the process started.

"They will be." Billy started toward the hall when Jasmine interrupted.

"Kids! We're leaving. You coming with us or walking?"

Jane tried to hide her smile as Billy hesitated, unsure whether to continue or wait on a response.

"Right, kids. Like your mother said." He shrugged and made a face.

Little Billy appeared first. "I can't tie this tie." He was in slacks and a dark shirt, unbuttoned, with a tie in his hand. One shoe was untied, and his fly was unzipped. Clearly there was more than just the tie holding him up.

Kathrine appeared, primped and perfect, with a smirk on her face. "He wanted me to tie it. I could, because I know how, but he wouldn't make my bed, so I wouldn't." She flounced self-righteously across the room to stand by Jane. "You're pretty, Grandma. I'm gonna stay beside you all evening."

"Pretty doesn't rub off, so give it up, squirt." Little Billy continued to twist at the tie, making no progress at all.

"Mom!"

"Be nice, kids. Now, to the car. We're all going in the XTS." Billy shooed them the direction of the front door.

"Can't we take Grandma's? It's red."

"And not big enough." Jasmine laid her brush on the entry console, picking up her purse. "Now, out, like your father said."

"Mom! My belt!" That was Little Billy.

"Here, Son." She pulled one out of her oversized handbag. "Out, now. No more excuses."

They tumbled out the door, and Jane watched them go by, three dressed to the nines, and the other barely dressed at all. However, they were hers, and she'd claim them all.

Before closing the door, she did look back in the mirror. Jasmine's earrings made all the difference in the world. She looked like a million bucks, which she assumed was about what Billy had paid for these. Having an architect for a stepson wasn't a bad thing, not in the least little bit.

"DRIVE ON, BILLY. You can't see the house until you're almost there." Jane motioned with her hand.

She sat in the front with her stepson, but she'd been amused by the antics in the back seat. Little Billy was in the middle, and both his sister and his mother had worked to get him polished to a shine. Jasmine had found a comb somewhere, wet it in a cup of water, and was smoothing his hair into a semblance of order.

"You did the drive, too?" There were flowering shrubs all the way from the road, and they lined the drive on both sides. The area underneath was mulched with pine needles and interspersed with beds of flowers.

"So the architect approves?" She sat back and smiled. She liked it. Cord had already given it his thumbs-up. But still, she'd needed to hear it from her family.

"You mean you designed all the outdoor plantings and structures?" Jasmine spoke from the back seat. "What about that cute gazebo we just passed?"

"That, too."

"I told you Grandma's smart." Katherine sounded very smug.

"You never said that," Little Billy snorted. "You said you didn't want to come. You'd rather play with your One Direction dolls."

"They're action figures, and I don't play with them. I take them on tour."

Billy cleared his throat. "Kids?"

Jane could tell it wasn't a question, and she was glad to have him corralling them. It got tiresome when she had to go it alone.

Thank God for parents!

"It doesn't matter, Little Billy. And, thank you, Katherine. I like being told I'm smart."

"See? Grandma loves me." Katherine waggled her shoulders. "Ha, ha."

"She loves to see you go home." Little Billy grabbed her knee and squeezed.

"Enough." Jasmine held out her hand to the pair as a signal to stop. "Be sweet just for an evening. This is an old friend of your grandmother's, and we want to impress him."

"Yeah," Katherine muttered. "Impress him."

"You can impress him," Little Billy muttered back, "by staying in the car."

Jane rolled her eyes, calling brightly, "We're here. Smiles, everyone." She opened her door as the car rolled to a stop.

They were in the drive, although they had passed a mowed area with signs and plastic ribbons showing visitors where to park.

"Mom, should I move the car after I let you out?" Billy glanced at the grassy parking area.

"Later, Son. We have two hours before the crowds arrive. There's time." Besides, she thought, she didn't know if the kids would survive that long. Billy and Jasmine might take them home long before the reunion began.

"Go ahead." Jasmine patted him on the shoulder. "You'll get a better parking spot. You can take the kids with you. The walk will be good for them."

"Thanks!" He rolled his eyes, but he was smiling. "Out, ladies. Stay, children."

"How long did it take you to do all this?" Jasmine glanced around at the lush landscape as the big luxury car pulled away.

"Not long enough. This was a six-month job, and I had to squeeze it into the past six weeks. The final landscaping just went in yesterday. So, you think I did okay?"

"Okay?"

Jane jumped. She recognized that voice, even as she refused to turn around.

"This is the most beautiful, or, should I say hermosa palace I've ever seen."

"Have we met?" Jasmine was the first to greet Cord.

"Two beautiful women, here in my own drive, speaking with me. Both of you are speaking with me, right, Jane?"

She turned to face him, to find his eyes glued on her. "What? Did I smear my lipstick?" She wanted to be beautiful. Now, under Cord's appraising eye, she felt nervous.

Jasmine giggled. "I don't think it's your lipstick."

"No, mi corazón, there's nothing wrong with you. You're perfect." Cord's eyes hadn't moved.

Billy was putting his key in his pocket as he appeared, motioning for the children to catch up. He gave Jasmine a hug.

"Who's he, Mom?" Jasmine let out another giggle.

"Excuse my bad manners. Jasmine, this is Juan Cordello Rivera the Third. He owns this ranch. Cord, this is my lovely and precious daughter-in-law, Jasmine." She was grateful to have her words not crack as she spoke them. She continued with the introductions, telling Cord each person with her.

When she finished, and everyone had nodded in all the right spots, Cord began to speak. "You have no idea how much your mother has done to this place.

There's nothing left of the old hacienda but the outer structure. She did all the design work on the casita and the patio as well as the hot tub. She even refinished the pool. She knew what I wanted even before I could tell her. She read my mind." Cord finished by putting his arm around Jane and squeezing her close to him. "Without her, this house would be nothing but a tired old part of the past blocking the landscape. But, because of her vision, my family home has come back to life again to be shared by the ones I love." When Cord finished, there were tears forming at the edges of his eyes.

Jane was embarrassed and flustered, and she could feel her hands shaking. For heaven's sake, why was he giving her so much attention? She'd been the director of the project, certainly, but to tell her family that his home wouldn't have existed without her? That was a surprise.

Yet, what amazed her more was that no one thought it odd that this stranger had his arm around her. And even more amazing, she didn't feel the desire to move away. Not quickly, anyway.

She knew she must, though. She felt very old and very uncomfortable feelings, and she knew they would make a complete fool of her.

There was no way she was telling this man she loved him, even though every part of her body screamed at her to do that very thing.

— 25 —

"SHALL WE TOUR the house?" Cord stood at Jane's side. His sudden appearance on the drive wasn't by chance, having been quite contrived. He was standing by the large windows in the front watching for her family's early arrival. He'd promised her son and daughter-in-law a private tour, after all. After yesterday, he'd wondered if she would show.

When she did emerge from the car, he hadn't been able to believe his eyes. She was by far the most captivating woman he'd ever seen, more beautiful than she'd been all those years ago.

"Let's start first by you leading on." Jane cleared her throat as she disentangled herself from his arm.

"If you'll walk by my side." He took her hand and bowed, kissing it. He refused to let her get away so easily. He smiled when he heard Katherine giggle.

"Grandma. You're a princess."

"You are, you know," Cord murmured. "You'll walk with me?"

"If I must."

He turned to the crowd. "You are my captive audience for the next two hours. Well," and he looked at his watch, "the next hour and fifty minutes. You're my first guests, and I wish to show off Jane's creation." He pulled her hand up and kissed it again. "Please pardon the kitchen. The caterers have commandeered that part of the house, so perhaps another day . . ." He looked at Jane, speaking softer. "You will come back another day?"

"Cord," she spoke low and tersely, "I'm finished here. You have your house back for you and your, um, other."

"My other?" He was amused. Clearly, she didn't understand. However, it was exactly how he'd planned today. "Never mind. You tell of your creation, and I'll clap and cheer."

He motioned for the others to gather around, and they headed for the front door. Cord did stop the boy, and he pulled him aside.

"Billy, right?"

The boy beamed. Jane had introduced him as Little Billy, and Cord thought maybe he'd enjoy a more grown-up name.

"Well, Billy, we have a saying out here on the ranch. When the gates are open, the cows like to wander and play."

Billy frowned. "What?"

Cord chuckled. "Your cows are getting out."

"Cows?"

Cord spelled it out. "Your zipper is undone, boy. Zip your pants." He patted him on the shoulder. "You can catch up with us when you're finished."

The boy turned bright red, but that was okay. Cord liked Jane's grandkids, and after spending the weekend with his own, they didn't seem very wild at all.

"THERE ARE GUESTS ARRIVING, and you're the host." The tour was over, and Jane pointed out the window, where two cars could be seen driving towards the house. They pulled off the drive, parking next to Billy's Cadillac.

"Yes, ma'am," Cord intoned wickedly. "Your wish is my command."

Jane laughed. "Stop that. You'd better be glad your Vangie isn't here to see you doing that."

He winked at her. "She would approve, I can assure you."

"I think not, and my grandkids are here. I don't approve."

He laughed and strode away, waving merrily at her family.

"Grandma, are you going to marry him?"

Jane rolled her eyes. "Katherine, you don't marry every man who kisses your hand."

"I would," she announced.

"And that's why you're a dork." Little Billy whispered the words in her ear.

"Mom!"

"Are you ready for us to go?" Billy stepped to his mother's side, while Jasmine corralled the disagreement. "One of us can come back to get you after this is over."

"No." She didn't want them to leave. She needed backup. She might even find the need to use the kids as her crutch. If Katherine did stick to her side, then that would be the witch hazel to ward off Cord's unwelcome advances.

This was turning out to be a complicated evening.

"If you're sure. I know my kids, Mom, better than perhaps even you. They can be toots, no question about it."

"We all have been, at one point or another. Let's give them a chance. I'll talk to them."

Jasmine had them corralled, and both of her grandkids had sour looks on their faces when Jane walked up to them.

"When was the last time you two ate anything?" She looked at them piercingly, and when she didn't get an answer, she spoke their parents. "You two go play. I'm taking these two to the kitchen. I think that's the problem." They were usually better than this in public. And she suspected they were very hungry. She knew she was.

She led them through the house to the back

entrance to the kitchen. She tapped a thin man in a white jacket on the shoulder.

"Sir, I have two hungry children here, and I'm afraid they're going to kill each other unless I get some food down them. Do you think you can rustle up something?" How easily the old ranching words came to her. She stifled a grin. She was a Texan, after all. Nothing to be ashamed of there.

"Yes, ma'am. Chicken, barbeque, or enchiladas?" He smiled pleasantly at her.

"You are a sweetheart." She smiled. "Let me check."

They walked away with two covered plates, and Jane carried two glasses of tea. Settling them in the dining room, one on each side of her, she drew in the aroma of the meal, chicken on one side, and barbeque on the other. The enchiladas had sounded more appealing to her, but she wasn't the one choosing. She would snack off the children's plates.

She did need tea, though.

"Children, I'll be right back. Grandma forgot her tea."

The two children nodded at her, more interested in their food than in their grandmother. On the way, she glanced outside to see a dozen more cars had arrived. Out back, people were gathering around the pool. With the evening, it would start to cool, and there couldn't be a better day for a high school reunion.

Then she caught the sounds of a brass instrument,

and she knew someone had hired a band. Mariachi, by the sound of the music. She smiled, heading back to her kids.

"Grandma, who is that man, really?" That was from Little Billy, finally asking a real question rather than tormenting his sister.

"An old friend. We dated in high school."

"Before you married Granddad Bill?" That was Katherine.

"Yes. A long time before."

"Why didn't you marry him?" Billy again.

"Oh, sometimes you don't marry the people you think you will. Then someone else comes along, and now I have you two wonderful children." She smiled brightly, giving each one a quick hug. "If I'd married that man, then I wouldn't have you, now would I?"

"Would you have had other kids?" Billy was licking his fingers, but he paused to look at her. "And I could have another sister that's not a *dork!*" That was aimed at his sister, and he leaned around to glare at her.

"Shush, Billy. Your sister isn't a dork." Besides, his comment hit close to home. Another sister ... well, not exactly a sister, but an aunt. Her daughter, Little Billy's aunt. She felt her eyes water, and she knew she couldn't let that get started. "All finished, here?" She stood. "Up, children. I have a reunion to attend."

"Will you be the prettiest person there? Here, I mean?"

Jane hugged Katherine and kissed her on the fore-head. "After you, I think so, dear. I certainly hope so."

"I saw a barn. Can we go explore?" Billy's eye's gleamed.

"A barn, Billy, in your tie and dress shoes?"

He shrugged. "Want to, Dork?"

"If you won't call me dork."

"Okay, Dorklet."

"Grandma!"

"Off, you two. No lights out there, so you have to get there while it's still light. I'll tell your parents." She patted them on the backsides as they scampered away, certain that they would argue, but maybe no one would hear them if they were in the barn.

"THANK YOU FOR THE nickel tour earlier." Jane had a glass of punch in her hand, and she'd seen Cord by himself during a lull. "What do you think of the mariachi band?"

"Lively. You know mi casa es su casa." He smiled at her.

"Not exactly, but I appreciate the sentiment."

"Ah, we have new guests." He motioned, and sure enough, two new couples strolled in together.

"I'll catch up with them later. I have to wait on name tags."

He whispered to her conspiratorially, "Me, too." He winked and walked off.

"Wow, Mom. You never mentioned him when

you talked about the remodel. I don't think I'd have been able to get much done with him around." Jasmine giggled.

"Oh, it's you, Jasmine!" Jane was started by her daughter-in-law's presence, and she felt her breath return. "I didn't know you were here. Are the kids back, yet?"

"Billy has them over at the horseshoes. They'll be okay for a while. I'm on break."

"You probably need it." Jane laughed softly. She's the one that needed a break, but that would happen about midnight when all this wound down. "So, you like my old boyfriend, do you?"

"Old boyfriend?"

"Very old, as in not seen for forty years. Now? He's got a girlfriend."

"Why didn't you snatch him up first? I would have."

"You've got Billy, but I understand what you mean. Bad blood." She laughed. "Just not bad enough to keep me from charging him an arm and a leg for redoing this place."

"Are you sure he has a girlfriend? He seems to have the hots for you, if I'm any reader of body language."

Jane looked at her, aghast. "The hots? Like romantic attraction? Heaven's, no! He told me himself he has a new love in his life, and I saw him coming out of J. Gale's the other day. So, I'm pretty sure I'm not the one for him." Her sarcastic tone told what she thought of that, she was certain.

"Oh. Sorry."

"Quite alright." The yard flickered, and festive lights erupted across the scene. "How pretty. Let's mingle." Jane smiled at Jasmine. They laughed to see several older teens come running out of the guesthouse and leap into the pool.

"Too bad the kids didn't bring their suits."

"Oh, I bet I could rustle up a few." There was that word again. Jane smiled. "Don't tell them yet, but I'll ask around."

"Hey, Jane! Is that you?"

She turned to see several men coming her way. She shrugged and waved at Jasmine, who smiled and walked away.

"You haven't changed a bit except to be even more gorgeous."

Not sure which one had spoken, Jane just smiled. An exceptionally handsome gentleman with a thickening middle approached her first.

"Oh, I know you." Jane laughed. "Yes, Romeo, it's me," she shot back with a short laugh. She remembered him. His last name was Romero, but he'd always been such a big flirt that the girls called him Romeo, a nickname he'd never liked.

"Give me a break, Jane. I've changed." He flashed a winning smile.

"And you've been divorced twice, or is it three times now?" Jane asked with an innocent smile, knowing good and well it was four.

"None of them were my fault, mi amor. I'm just looking for true love. A woman I can trust. Someone who doesn't gripe all the time if I make a little mistake now and then. A little indiscretion is to be expected by a man."

"You wish!"

"You never gave me a chance in high school; you were so wrapped up in Tarzan. Now, maybe it's our turn." Romeo blew her a kiss as he waited for her response.

Jane just laughed and patted his arm as she turned away. She saw Cord across the pool, and she waved to him, calling, "Suits? Do you have extras?"

He smiled broadly. "You want to go in?"

"No, fool!" She motioned him over, meeting him halfway. "I have grandkids who might like to. I don't want to get their hopes up, though."

"In the casita. Veronica brought a dozen extra."

"Just for girls?"

He laughed. "Boys, also. Tell your grandkids to make themselves at home."

She did, and they did, soon frolicking in the water, and more importantly, occupied. Now if they didn't drown one another, but as they had a pool at home, and neither one was deceased yet, she was certain they would survive.

It was sitting down to dinner that she got a surprise. Each guest had registered upon arrival, and someone had made out cards for seating. When she found hers, it was right next to Cord's. Just as Jane reached for her seat, a hand came around, and a deep voice spoke.

"Allow me."

"Did you do this?" She didn't even have to look to know it was Cord. Somehow, he'd managed to invade the most intimate part of the evening and sit by her. "I suppose since the party's at your house, you get to call some of the shots."

"Me? I'm innocent."

"I doubt that."

"Do not break my heart, mi corazón. I only wish you to have a good time." He bowed to her slightly.

She doubted that, and she found his behavior very confusing. It didn't help that his proximity to her tonight put her stomach in knots. She'd thought she would be able to enjoy this evening, but she'd been seriously mistaken. Anywhere Cord was, her heart wouldn't leave her alone. Right now, it was pounding against her ribcage like it was about to escape.

"Aren't you going to eat, Jane? The meat's from my herd of prize Angus. I donated the beef for the party. I can't speak for the chicken." He leaned in close, his words whispered in her ear.

As she turned to reply, she happened to notice that she and Cord were wearing identical colors of fabric. The pearl snaps on his shirt were the same as the sequins on her dress. His bolo tie had a huge piece of sapphire surrounded by turquoise. The large stone matched her sequins perfectly. It was as if they had planned their outfits together.

"Is something wrong?"

"It's your shirt and tie. They match my outfit perfectly," Jane mumbled under her breath, not entirely comforted by the observation.

"Well, it's a small world, and even smaller when the choices are limited in this community." He grinned broadly. "What do you think about that?"

She didn't want to think about it at all.

— 26 —

THE EVENING WAS IN full swing. Dusk had over-
taken the hills in the distance, the sun winking out
like an orange fist that had held the day tightly in its
grasp, only releasing its hold as it disappeared from
sight. The darkness flooded in, suddenly complete.

Yet, around the hacienda's pool, the mariachi music was lively, and the brightly-colored globes of the
party lights glittered like colored diamonds. Dancers
twirled or swayed to the music, whatever happened to
suit their mood, some very near the swimmers in the
pool.

Nothing suited Jane's mood. Neither had the three
bites of beef she'd eaten, or the sopapilla she'd
choked down. She was irritated at Cord. He'd commandeered her as his seating partner, and now he had

disappeared to heaven knew where.

Jane looked around as the music changed, picking up in beat, and strobe lights started to flash. She'd forgotten. The DJ. One had been hired for the final part of the festivities.

"Ma'am, your things? Are you finished?"

A young man in a white apron indicated her empty plate. Her glass was still half full, but she smiled and motioned. "Take it all. I'm finished."

"We'll be clearing away the tables soon. You may want to join the others around the pool. The dance floor will be going here."

"Oh! My! I had no idea we were going all out." She laughed, but it was to charm the boy. She was really concerned that Billy and the rest of the family were nowhere to be seen. She glanced in the pool, but there were no familiar faces, and no bodies on the bottom. She had no idea where everyone had gone.

It was the dance floor that got her attention. A gridwork frame was snapped together on the grass, then a hardwood floor was unrolled in three sections and pinned in place with stakes. Just like that. The first person she saw step out was Romeo. For a minute he was by himself, dancing in the colored strobe lights. Then he saw her and motioned for her to come on out.

She laughed. Why not? She kicked off her shoes and stepped onto the wood surface, taking his hand. The first thing he did was spin her around and drop her in his arms.

"You're entirely too beautiful, mi amor. What does Tarzan have that I don't?" He whispered the words to her.

When he pulled her up, she winked, and with a smile, she said, "It's what you do have."

"What's that?" He looked puzzled.

"Four divorces."

"Uh!" He frowned. "Does everyone know?"

Jane laughed. "Of course. This is a very small town."

"Want to try for number five?" He was all smiles again.

By that time there were several other couples on the floor with them, and Jane asked to be released. She had done her duty, and as she picked up her shoes and put them on, she looked back to the dance floor. There was Cord.

She suddenly felt sick. He was with some woman she didn't recognize. She was entirely too young for Cord, but she had a huge diamond on her finger.

The engagement ring Cord had purchased at J. Gale's. It was on her finger. It must be. No one that young could afford a ring like that! She must be Cord's fiancée, Vangie.

"Oh, Billy, where are you?" She wanted desperately to leave this party. She looked for Peggy and couldn't find her, either. She reached for an arm she recognized. "Roxi?" It was Roxanne Fuller, although Jane knew she'd married and now had a different last name. "Have you seen Peggy?"

"Peggy Johnson?"

"I can't find her anywhere, and she's my ride home." She would be, too, if Billy and Jasmine had already made their exit.

"Jane, honey, I think she was at the little building over there, earlier. That, what did Cord call it, his *Casa di Sita?*" Roxanne grinned. "I don't think that was it, but close, anyway."

"Sure. Thanks, Roxi. I'll check there." What she would do was head to the house. Her handbag was inside—a blue clutch, very tiny—and her phone was in the bag. She'd start calling numbers, and she'd find out where someone was, a taxi, if nothing else.

Inside she located her clutch and pulled out her phone. Scrolling through her numbers, she walked to the French doors facing on the festivities. Cord and his "girl" stepped off the dance floor, laughing. Jane let her phone drop. Surely this wasn't Vangie. Now that she saw her full in the face, she definitely had the Rivera look, especially in her smile. And she couldn't be over thirty-five, although with modern skin care, she could possibly be nearer forty.

She must be one of Cord's nieces. Yes, that was it. Relief flooded over Jane. The girl was one of Cord's nieces, and she'd joined the party because she could. After all, this was her uncle's home.

Even so, Jane had reached her limit. The quiet of the house was nice. Peggy could have her good time for a while longer. Jane would run her down later, if Billy and Jasmine didn't show.

As she walked back toward the living room, she heard one of the French doors open with a whoosh, and a voice called to her.

"Jane! I thought I saw you inside. I have someone I want you to meet." It was Cord, half in and half outside the house.

"Not now, Cord. I'm about partied out." She waved tiredly. "I'm sitting through this one."

"Oh, no, you're not." He grinned. "You want to meet this person."

She drew in a sharp breath, retorting, "Sure, if I must. Let's get this over with."

Cord turned and motioned someone to join him. He pushed the door wider, and the young woman he'd been dancing with stepped in with a smile.

"Hello," she said.

"Pleased to meet you." *And to get a ride home,* but Jane kept that inside. This was one girl she didn't care to meet, niece or fiancée. But, she was here, trapped, and she could be polite.

Cord took a deep breath and said, "Jane, this is Vangie. Her full name is Evangeline Joy Wise. Vangie, this is Katherine Jane Lane."

"Waggoner." Jane corrected the inaccuracy, nodding politely. "Jane Waggoner. Lane is my maiden name."

"This is so exciting." Vangie rubbed her arms, and she giggled. "I have been waiting all my life to meet you."

"All your life?" Jane frowned, caught off guard.

"Cord, maybe you should explain to me."

"I'm sorry." Vangie looked at Cord and held up a finger. "You don't know, yet. I don't guess Dad has told you. I forgot that this was a surprise." She giggled again, in a way that seemed very familiar to Jane. Her voice, too. Familiar, and yet not at all.

"I don't know what? Cord?" Dad? Jane felt her head tighten, and she clutched her phone tighter. A lifeline. It was her lifeline to rescue. Peggy, Billy, a taxi. Someone. Anyone.

"Let me." Vangie stepped to Jane and put her arms out. "I want to hug you. Is that okay?"

Jane stood frozen, but she didn't say no.

In the hug, Vangie whispered, "Thank you for loving me enough to give me a chance at life." She backed away, still holding to Jane, as she whispered with a smile and tears, "Mom."

Jane felt the room go silent. She couldn't take it in. Then, she felt her knees give way, and everything went black.

"JANE?"

She looked up to find Cord's face over her, and his hand holding hers. "Did I dream that?"

"Your daughter? No, she's right here beside me." He chuckled. "We didn't mean to scare you to death."

"Are you all right, Mom?" The voice that was so familiar, and yet not familiar at all, enveloped her.

"Could I get some water? My mouth, it's dry." She pulled herself up and into a chair, looking to see

Vangie heading off into the next room. "Cord, are you serious?" She nodded Vangie's direction.

"Serious as all get-out." He had an insane grin on his face.

"Where did she come from?"

"Oh, Jane, after all this time, you can't figure that out?" He laughed. "You, girl, have a lot to learn, if you don't know where babies come from."

— Epilogue —

"AND THAT'S HOW IT all happened up to right now." Vangie finished with a hug and a smile for Jane, having told of the thirteen years she'd spent with her adopted parents in Brazil, and their death on a supply trip home to the States when their single engine plane crashed.

Jane patted her face with a tissue. It was really too much to take in. "Cord, you couldn't tell me about this six weeks ago?"

"Would you have listened six weeks ago?"

"And you and Shelly?" This part still had Jane puzzled. After all, he did marry the woman.

"Remember, Jane? I tried to tell you. Veronica was born very premature. Except she was over eight pounds. I was a kid. I didn't know, so I accepted it."

"How much premature?"

"Two months. Her birthday is in December. It makes sense, if you think about it."

"And you never figured it out." Jane was still having trouble taking it all in. Vangie was her daughter, adopted by a young couple killed while traveling on the mission field.

"As I said, I was a kid."

"She tricked you." It sounded like Shelly.

"That's as good a way to say it as any. My family had a good name, and hers had threatened to throw her out. That party was her chance. And they didn't have DNA testing back then." He shook his head resignedly. "But that's over and done with."

"And you figured this out how?"

"A hand-written note from Shelly. It was in her desk from years ago. I don't think she remembered writing it, and at the end, she was so sick, she probably didn't care."

"But," Jane hesitated, "that doesn't explain you." She spoke to Vangie. "How did you find us?"

"I didn't." She had pulled up a chair for Cord and for herself by that time. "That was Veronica's doing."

"So, let me get this straight." Jane didn't think she had it straight at all, but she would give it a shot. "Veronica figured out her father and a woman she'd never met had a daughter in South America that had been adopted to a couple on the mission field?" She laughed. "No one's going to believe that. I'm having trouble with it, myself."

"No, it was simpler. Veronica and I have talked it through the past few days. It was the note from her mother." Vangie looked at Cord, suppressing a smile. "When Dad showed her, she was so excited. She'd known they were nothing alike. The note explained something she'd suspected for years. She started researching, and she found her birth father's records. He was a pilot killed in Vietnam less than a year after she was born. The grandparents on that side were gone, also. There was only a third cousin left, or something like that. That was how she confirmed the details. The cousin died shortly after, so that connection is gone forever."

"However," Cord broke in, "that wasn't all she found. Me, on some paperwork with a K. J. Lane. Hm. Wonder who that could be?" He grinned. "And you didn't even tell me."

Now it was Jane's turn to be on the spot. "Self-preservation. I tried to hide it, telling my parents I was in Denton at college. Really, I was in the Esther House for pregnant girls. Your birthday is Valentine's, right?"

Vangie nodded. "Your parents never knew they had a granddaughter?"

"Perhaps." Jane felt guilty about that. "I think they knew something. They treated me as if I should be guilty of something, but we never talked about it. But then, that was my family. We either yelled at each other or swept things under the rug." She felt the tears break through her veneer of self-control. "I hope you had a happy childhood. I truly tried to do what was best for you. I had nothing to offer you with me being so young, and my parents would have been ashamed."

Vangie grabbed her mother and held her close, patting her arm. "Oh, don't worry one bit about me. I had the best life ever. It was all part of God's great plan. He took something that was meant to be for bad and turned it for good. That's the way God is."

"And they were killed on a supply run, you said, in an airplane?" Even for a Christian, that didn't sound so good.

"Yes." Vangie's eyes were red. "But I know where they are. They're with the Heavenly Father."

"But since then, how did you manage?" Jane felt a twinge of guilt that she'd been unable to let go of the simple things God had been dealing with in her devotions. Forgive. Forget. Don't get angry. Love. And this girl had struggled with the premature death of her parents. How sad.

"I was twenty-five when that happened. I stayed there a couple more years until a new missionary family could be trained and placed there.

"I came back to the States and finished my doctoral studies in counseling. Then I worked in various facilities. Last year, I met Jeremiah Cowling, a wonderful doctor at one of the hospitals where I worked. We share the same faith and commitment to God and the hurting world around us. We became engaged and are getting married next month. He tried to come with me to the reunion, but there was an emergency sur-gery he had to perform just as we were readying to leave.

"We want to start a family of our own as soon as possible, but we also plan on adopting, as well. I'm here this evening hoping my father will give me away, and my mother will be my matron of honor."

"Did you know you were adopted when you were growing up?" That question had haunted Jane for years.

"Of course. My parents always told me that most parents didn't get to choose their children, but they picked me, and I was loved more because I was adopted." She smiled. "I loved it that I was adopted. I felt sorry for kids that weren't."

"You never wanted to look for us?"

"I didn't want to intrude. You did the greatest thing of all by letting me live. I had great parents. Now I believe God wants me to be a part of your lives."

Cord wiped his eyes and asked, "Would you be opposed to a double ceremony?"

"Double ceremony? Who are you marrying?" Jane felt her heart drop.

Cord reached into his pocket and pulled out a vel-vet ring box from J. Gale's Fine Jewelry Store. He opened it to reveal a five-carat heart-shaped diamond mounted on a platinum band. He carefully took Jane's hands in his. "I've always loved you, and only you, Jane. Will you marry me and make me the most blessed man on the face of the earth?"

"You want to marry me?" Jane had to get her head around this. Her daughter was back, Cord knew what Jane had done, and now he wanted to propose. She could barely speak. "After all this?"

"Yes, and I want an answer now, tonight, before another crazy thing happens. I want to know that you love me and want me to be your husband for the rest of your life." He knelt at her side. "I lost you for forty years. I can't lose you again, mi corazón."

"Yes." She felt her voice tremble, and as she said the word, she knew she meant it with every ounce of her being. "Absolutely yes." She shook as he slipped the ring on her finger.

"It's beautiful." Vangie took her hand.

"Does it fit?" From Cord.

"I think so. How . . ."

"Let me just say Peggy's a really good friend," Cord chuckled. "I had to get it re-sized. I'd just come out of the store with it when I saw you the other day. It was a close call. I thought maybe you knew something was up."

Jane was secretly glad he didn't know she thought he was in there buying an engagement ring for Vangie.

Cord let go of Jane's hands, and he stood up and yelled toward the bedroom, "You can all come out now. She said yes!"

Out of Cord's bedroom poured Veronica and her husband, along with the boys, and then Billy, Jasmine, their children, and finally, Peggy. They all ran up at once and began hugging everyone.

"You mean everyone knew about this but me?"

Billy piped up, "Veronica called me about a month ago with the news. I think it's going to be great to have sisters to share the holidays with."

Jasmine smiled in approval.

Then, Peggy broke in, "I only found out this week because everyone was afraid I'd tell you." She tried to look like she was pouting, but it only produced more laughter and giggles.

Cord spoke up, "When I finally found our daughter a little over a year ago, it was all I could do not to call and tell you right then. But it wasn't the right timing for Vangie. So, I waited."

Vangie laughed and said, "You know what they say: The mother is always the last to know."

Cord finally reminded everyone there was a party going on outside, and he'd better attend to it.

Jane followed him out the door to see what his next step would be. From now on, she planned to be at his side. She was still in a state of elation and shock to know she was finally going to be with the man of her dreams. She had to agree with Vangie that only God could have pulled off something this spectacular.

Cord stepped outside onto the patio and walked over to the DJ booth. He turned off the CD that was playing and asked for the microphone. The surprised DJ quickly obliged.

"Ladies and gentlemen, I have an announcement

to make." Cord paused for a moment for the crowd to settle so they could hear his news. Various friends and classmates looked at one another as if trying to figure out what would be so important. "I want you to know that on our fortieth class reunion, Jane has finally said yes to Tarzan. I'll no longer be swinging through the trees alone, but will have at my side our classmate and the love of my life, Jane. Our three children are here to celebrate this wonderful occasion and the uniting of our families."

Friends in the crowd cheered and hooted, while others looked puzzled, trying to figure out the "three children" part. Cord just smiled as he walked off stage and grabbed Jane around the waist, pulling her close to him.

All she said was, "Bring it on, Tarzan."